STELLA AND THE
YELLOW CELLO

PETER GALE

CENTAUR PRESS
an imprint of OPEN GATE PRESS
LONDON

Published in 2014 by Centaur Press,
an imprint of Open Gate Press
51 Achilles Road, London NW6 1DZ

British Library Cataloguing-in-Publication Programme
A catalogue reference for this book is available from the
British Library.

ISBN: 978-0-900001-63-5

Printed and bound in Great Britain by Imprint Digital, Exeter, Devon

Stella has reminded me that I must give a special word of thanks to Catherine Leopold for her invaluable editorial expertise.

CONTENTS

PART 1   1

1.   Games, Jokes and Novelties   3
2.   The Richest Little Girl in the World   10
3.   Cellos Can't Walk   16
4.   Call Me Stella   22
5.   The Monster   30
6.   Sandy Bottom   35
7.   Batty and Dottie   40
8.   A Dream Donkey   46
9.   A Dream Cello   53
10.   First the Good News   60
11.   The Awful, Terrible Truth   70
12.   The Fabulous Cripes Diamond   78
13.   Unlucky For Some   84
14.   Royal Connections   89
15.   Lethal Ice   96

PART 2   105

16. First the Bad News   107
17. And Now For The Really Bad News   114
18. Stella Goes PING   126
19. Stella Has Mail   137
20. Something For Nothing   147
21. Thunder And Lightning   157
22. Surprise Surprise   165
23. It Was Like This   169
24. A Curse and a Coincidence   179

PART ONE

CHAPTER ONE

Games, Jokes and Novelties

'Is this it?' exclaimed Stella.

'Yes.'

'A yellow cello? You must be joking. You can *not* be *serious!*'

Mr Beeswax looked at her sharply over his spectacles.

'I assure you I am not joking,' he said quietly. 'The cello is yellow and it is yours.'

'I can *see* it's yellow,' Stella snapped, 'and I don't *want* it!'

She was sitting at her very grand desk, in her very grand study, facing the solicitor.

As for the offending cello, it was leaning against a bookcase, as if to say, 'Nice place you've got here.'

The solicitor took off his reading glasses. He peered at Stella again, even more sharply.

'Little girl –' he began.

'Don't you little girl me,' Stella interrupted crossly.

'That's precisely what you are. A little girl – a very rude and difficult little girl.'

'All the best people are rude and difficult. That's why they're in the newspapers. They're celebrities who are successful and famous. And *rich!*' She leaned forward. 'Like *me!*' she shouted in his face.

What a strange way to start a story – two people having a row about a yellow cello. Or was it about being rich?

Mr Beeswax waited in silence for Stella to calm down. But she didn't.

'Do you know how rich I am?' she asked, scowling.

Mr Beeswax smiled at her as if it was a stupid question.

'Do you think that's a stupid question?'

3

'Yes and no.'

'What do you mean, yes and no?'

'Yes, I think it's a stupid question, and, no, I don't know how rich you are,' he replied, putting his glasses on again. 'But at a rough guess I'd say you were a darn sight too rich for your own good.'

His calm, cutting reply left her temporarily dumbstruck. Normally, no one dared to talk back at her like that.

She was only a little girl and small for her age, but she bossed everyone about like a bearded tyrant in ancient times. Except that she didn't have a beard, of course.

Mr Beeswax was a very capable solicitor, with a quiet manner, who tended to drop things at important moments. This was one of them.

'Now if you'll allow me to perform my duty,' he said, and several papers fell to the floor. This pleased Stella no end. She laughed as he bent to pick them up.

'I'm instructed to inform you, forthwith, that a person by the name of Olive Underfelt died recently. There is no forwarding address. She was an eccentric lady who lived alone in a remote lighthouse, and she left you this cello, which is yellow, as you see.'

'I *know* it's yellow! How many times are you going to *repeat* that fact? What do I want with a stupid yellow cello? This is a complete waste of my time! I thought you were going to bring me something valuable, like a solid gold cake stand.'

'Yes, Stella, I'm sure you did. I was warned that you take after your father. He would have expected something valuable too. However, this cello is now yours and my duty is fulfilled. Forthwith.'

And with that Mr Beeswax put his spectacles away, collected his papers, placed them in his briefcase and walked out of Stella's study.

His coolness disappointed Stella. In fact, it made her boil. She enjoyed needling and infuriating people, watching their faces go bright red, hearing them stammer and struggle to find the right words.

She jumped out of her chair. 'If I ever see him again, I'll really aggravate him. I'll make him shake all over and swell up like a balloon and choke, and smack his hand on the table so hard he'll yell with pain. He will! *He will!*'

And she stamped her foot, forgetting she was wearing no shoes and had left her roller-skates nearby. Her foot hit one of the skates and *she* was the one who yelled with pain.

'Ow-ow-ow-ow-ow-ow!'

There was a timid knock on the door.

'Come in!' she bawled, rubbing her foot and blinking back tears of pain. A thin, middle-aged lady with large, anxious eyes entered the room.

'What's the matter, Stella? Have you hurt yourself?'

'Don't fuss over me, Aunt Zany, for heaven's sake.'

'Mr Beeswax looked very stern as he left.'

'He's a gruesome old gherkin.'

'Is this what he brought you? A lovely cello?' Aunt Zany murmured sweetly. 'How very unusual. It's yellow.'

Stella scowled at her. 'Don't *you* start.'

'What have I done wrong now?'

'Don't tell me that cello is yellow. I *know* it's yellow!'

And she stamped her foot again, this time hitting the corner of the desk.

'Ow-ow-ow-ow-ow-ow!'

Aunt Zany thought it best to leave her unhappy niece alone.

She moved about the room, looking for things to tidy up. As she bent down to pick up the roller-skates, she made a curious noise. Rattle-rattle.

'Aunt Zany, you're getting louder than ever.'

'Am I? I can't help it. It's all these pills I have to take.'

'It sounds awful – like pebbles in a cardboard box. You must try to stop it. People who come to the house think there's something wrong with their ears.'

'Oh dear. I'm so sorry.' Rattle-rattle. 'Tell me, how do you like your new cello?' she asked, trying to draw Stella's attention away from her rattling problem.

'I don't. Who was Olive Underfelt?' Stella sulked.

'Olive Underfelt,' her aunt repeated nervously. 'Should I know her?'

'The crazy lady in the lighthouse.'

'Oh her! Oh, she was just a distant relative, several times removed, if not more. She lived all alone, poor soul, with only her cello and a parrot for company.'

'Who got the parrot?'

'I don't know.'

'I wish she'd given *me* the parrot instead of that stupid-looking thing,' Stella grumbled, casting an unkind look at the cello. Which only goes to show that, however rich people are, they are never satisfied.

'I think Mr Beeswax was a little upset because you kept him waiting for two hours in your study. I'm sure he's a busy man.'

'Well I'm busy too, Aunt Zany. And when you're as rich as I am, you can do anything you want.'

To which Aunt Zany felt there was no reply.

'Can you play the cello, Aunt Zany? It's yours if you want it. For a reasonable price.'

Aunt Zany tugged at the brown mittens covering her knuckles.

'Not with my painful arthritic fingers. No, I don't play any instruments at all,' she said sadly.

Just then, the maid arrived to vacuum the carpet. She was a pretty girl of seventeen called Isabel Tinklin, and it was her first day working in Stella's luxury London home overlooking Regent's Park.

She noticed the cello leaning in the corner.

'Oh, what an unusual cello,' she remarked, trying to be friendly. 'It's yellow.'

Stella was eating an apple. She went stiff with fury and bit her tongue.

'Ow-ow-ow-ow-ow-ow!'

'What's wrong?' asked Isabel. 'I only said it was yellow.'

'You're fired!' Stella shouted.

As Isabel crept out of the room sobbing quietly, Aunt Zany quietly muttered, 'I can't cope. I just can't cope.'

Poor Aunt Zany. What a character! What a case! The answer to all her problems was pills. Pills by the bottle, by the dozen, by the fistful.

When she went to bed she took Sleeping Pills. When she went to keep-fit classes she took Leaping Pills. When she did the spring-cleaning she took Sweeping Pills and when she cried at funerals she took Weeping Pills.

'I don't know what I'd do without them,' she would say. 'It's my nerves.' But she might have taken fewer pills if Stella hadn't been so difficult to live with.

Stella was telling the truth when she said she was very rich. She was the only daughter of a multi-millionaire, Ivor Wishbone, who had acquired his vast fortune by running a company called

GAMES, JOKES AND NOVELTIES!
Tee Hee Hee! Ha Ha Ha!

We sell masks that turn you into
Monsters, Ghosts, Robots and Clowns!
Axes and Arrows that seem to go right through your head!
Button-Hole Flowers that squirt water in people's eyes!
Cushions that make rude noises when you sit on them!
Laughably popular!
Dog Poo made of brown plastic
– the last thing people want to find
on their newly cleaned carpet!
Spectacles that make your eyes spring out of their sockets!
Ridiculously amusing!
Chattering False Teeth, Itching Powder, Invisible Ink,
Stink Bombs
and Mugs that dribble down your front!
Absurdly hilarious!
Leaky Pens, Jig-saw Puzzles, Yo-yo's, Hula-Hoops,
Skate-Boards and many, many more!
Treat yourself and your friends to hours of fun and laughter.
Tee Hee Hee! Ha Ha Ha!

The strange thing was that Stella's father had no sense of humour at all. He was a miserable, sour-faced man who had never been known to smile or make a joke.

One day an eager young man called Percy Veer turned up with some large printed cards he wanted to sell.

'I call them *Playful Pranks For Perky People*.'

He held up the first one –

7

DO NOT USE TOILET
WET PAINT

'It would cause hours of uproarious inconvenience in a crowded office with only one toilet.'

'Most amusing,' Mr Wishbone commented, in his dull, lifeless voice. 'Not what I'm looking for.'

The young man presented another card.

COFFEE MACHINE OUT OF ORDER
DO NOT SWITCH ON

'This would have factory workers in fits of laughter!' the young man claimed merrily.

'Very funny,' Mr Wishbone muttered. 'Not what I'm looking for.'

Percy Veer showed him a third card.

WINDOW UNSAFE
DO NOT OPEN

'On a boiling hot day, this would really raise a giggle.'

'Highly droll but no thank you.'

As he left his office that evening, Mr Wishbone complained to his secretary, Penny Whistle.

'I do wish these people wouldn't bother me. They never come up with anything original.'

'Shocking,' Miss Whistle said, smiling sympathetically, but thinking, 'You stingy old creep. You always say, *'Not what I'm looking for,'* then you go and pinch their ideas.'

'Goodnight, Miss Whistle.'

'Nice weekend, Mr Wishbone.'

His office was on the twentieth floor of a tall glass block.

When he reached the lift, he found a printed notice stuck on the door. It said –

DANGER
LIFT NOT WORKING.
USE STAIRS

'Nice try,' he commented, dryly. 'But I never fall for practical jokes.'

He removed the notice and pressed the button.

'Quite comic, though,' he muttered. 'I'll use this idea.'

The doors opened. Still examining the card closely, he stepped into the empty elevator shaft.

It was a posh funeral, not well attended.

And there were no jokes.

CHAPTER TWO

The Richest Little Girl in the World

Stella had inherited her father's entire fortune. It was immense.
    In his will, Mr Wishbone had written –
'In the event of my death, my only child Stella will take over complete and absolute control of my worldwide company and investments. Let me make this totally clear. Very young she may be, but I want her to manage all my business and financial interests single-handedly. To this end, she has been taught by an expert in money matters. Me. She will know exactly what to do. I have taken this precaution to stop any crafty Trustees getting their greedy paws on my cash. Stella is both clever and wise. She will make an excellent businesswoman.'
    But he was wrong.
    There is a big difference between being clever and being wise. You could say, for example, that to spin round on one leg twenty times without stopping (like a brilliant ballet dancer) is clever. But to do so in the path of an oncoming express train would not be wise. Stella was certainly clever as far as business matters were concerned, but was she wise? Time would tell.

It was Aunt Zany who broke the news to Stella of her father's sudden death.
    Stella frowned. 'In that case, sell ninety percent of my shares in British Balloons. The market is about to burst.'
    'But Stella, aren't you upset?'
    'What about?'
    'That you'll never see your father again.'
    'I never saw him when he was alive. He taught me how to run

the firm, but after that he was mostly away. I just got postcards and emails every so often. Oh, and get my Loaded Dice Company on the phone. They need shaking up.'

Stella was now as busy as her father had been. And it has to be admitted, she had a wonderful head for business, in spite of her young age. And a tendency to fire people all the time.

Her mornings were spent with private tutors, keeping up her school lessons. After lunch she studied management reports and financial newspapers. She then held important meetings via the internet with business associates at her London office.

In the evenings she looked at new Games, Jokes and Novelties which her staff in Creative Personnel had dreamed up – spacemen masks, 3-D puzzles, false vampire fangs, kites, computer games and quiz books.

She had to examine them all thoroughly before giving the go-ahead for their mass production. She discovered that testing objects for their 'fun value' was not much fun. In fact, by the end of the day she was worn out.

But even when she went to bed, a good night's sleep was hardly possible. She was woken up by several urgent phone calls from her representatives in New York, Melbourne or Hong Kong, where it was the middle of the day or late afternoon. The result was that Stella was always tired and bad tempered. Did she complain? She never stopped.

'This weather is horrible.'

'I hate that colour.'

'Those shoes are rubbish.'

'I'm really fed up.'

'People are annoying.'

'I'm freezing. Shut the window.'

'It's boiling in here. Turn off the heating.'

It was beyond Aunt Zany to cope with her.

'If your mother were still alive,' Aunt Zany said one morning at breakfast, 'she would stop you working so hard.'

Stella often wondered about her mother. There were no photographs of her in the house and her father had seldom referred to her, except to say that she had died when Stella was born and it had broken his heart.

'You ought to get out in the fresh air and play games with other children,' suggested Aunt Zany. 'I know! Why don't we throw a lovely tea-party for all the boys and girls who live along the street?'

'What a revolting idea. Please, Aunt Zany, not while I'm eating my scrambled eggs.'

'But you shouldn't spend your whole day in the company of grown-ups. It's not healthy.'

'I *hate* children,' Stella declared firmly. 'They're so – how can I put it? – so childish.'

'Of course they're childish. They're children!' Aunt Zany protested, to no effect.

'Well, I find grown-ups much more – what's the word? – grown-up. Now please, may we change the subject? The thought of a tea-party with a heap of horrid, sticky kids makes me feel quite sick.' And she began to read the morning paper.

'I can't cope. I just can't cope,' murmured Aunt Zany, as she popped a handful of red and green pills into her mouth, and then washed them down with a cup of tea.

Suddenly, Stella shouted at the top of her voice, 'Mammoth mega-mergers!! It's *me!!*'

Aunt Zany was so surprised, she gave a loud burp, followed by a quick rattle.

'Pardon,' she said, and blushed hotly.

'Look, in this paper. It's a picture of me. And underneath my photograph there's a caption. It says:

Stella Wishbone (above)
Probably the richest girl in the world.'

'How nice,' Aunt Zany remarked.

'What do they mean, "probably"? I *am* the richest girl in the world. I wish they'd get their facts right. Then it says:

When her father died, she inherited
an orphanage in Pimlico.'

'PING,' exclaimed Aunt Zany.

'You're making some very peculiar noises this morning, Aunt Zany.'

'No, Stella. If I may explain, PING stands for the Peckham Institute for the Nervous and Gifted. It was built as an orphanage in 1750, but now it's a boarding school for clever children who can't afford expensive schooling.'

'How on earth did my father come to own it?'

'The building belonged to a penniless widow who owed him money. She gave it to him in lieu of cash. I remember, when he accepted it, he said, *'I consider this a very generous act on my part.'* Of course, the land alone is worth a fortune. His idea was to tear the whole place down one day and build a multi-storey car park there.'

Aunt Zany shuddered as she spoke. Rattle, rattle.

'But he didn't, so where's the return? Where's the income?'

'The school pays a rent.'

'How much?' Stella asked, beadily.

'Five pence a year.'

'A piffling pepper-corn rent! I'll have to raise it.'

'But Stella, you can't.'

'I can do anything I want, because I'm rich,' Stella pointed out simply.

'But it's run by a charity. They can't pay you more. They're struggling to make ends meet as it is. They'd have to close down. Think of the children!' Aunt Zany pleaded, trembling all over.

'I told you – thinking of children makes me feel sick. OK, how about this? I'll install a hundred video game machines at 50p a go. All the dear little kiddy-winkies will get hooked on playing them and I'll make a juicy profit.'

'But the children have no money. They come from poor families. They're nervous and gifted. That's why they need the school.'

'Well, they'll have to be nervous and gifted somewhere else. I'm selling it. Put a FOR SALE advert in the papers.'

'That's your secretary's job, Stella. Where is she?'

'I fired her.'

'But that's the fifteenth this year! And it's only February!'

'She had a silly face.'

'Dee Pendybull had excellent references.'

'Another one's coming tomorrow,' Stella said, standing up. 'I'm flying to Paris for a meeting this afternoon. Find out who Olive Underfelt left her parrot to. See if they'll swap it for that useless cello. I don't want it to be here when I get back.'

And off she marched for her morning lessons.

Oh yes, Stella Wishbone was certainly rich. She owned two jet planes – a pale blue one and a bright pink one.

When her morning lessons were over, she ran upstairs to change her clothes and phone her chief air pilot.

'Get the blue plane ready. I'm flying to Paris this afternoon and I've decided to wear my faded denim outfit.'

'Right away, Miss.'

Oh yes, Stella was definitely rich. Her large London house contained a swimming pool, a cinema and a bowling alley, none of them ever used.

Her cupboards were crammed with expensive bags and shoes of every shape and colour, and her closets were bursting with coats, scarves, hats, gloves, watches, belts, badges, beads and bangles – often worn only once and then thrown onto the pile, never to see the light of day again.

Having changed, Stella was about to leave her bedroom when she caught sight of the yellow cello leaning in a dark corner of the room. She stood absolutely still.

How odd. Was it her imagination, or was the cello looking at her? Stella blinked and rubbed her eyes. Yes, it seemed to be gazing directly at her. And smiling!

At that moment, the sun came out and filled the room with brilliant colours. All the gloomy shadows disappeared and the smile melted away.

No, it was just a trick of the light. Cellos can't smile. Can they?

As Stella settled into the deeply cushioned chair on her pale blue plane, she picked up the phone that connected her with her pilot, Heath Rowe.

'OK, let's go to Paris. Oh, and by the way, I left my sunglasses at home, the ones with the tartan frames. Ring Aunt Zany. Tell her I want them flown over to me in Paris, pronto. In the pink jet.'

'Yes, Miss.'

'How on earth do people cope with only one plane?' she asked.

'I can't imagine, Miss. You may like to know that it's raining in Paris, Miss.'

'I always wear my tartan shades at business meetings,' she snapped. 'It confuses people.'

'Yes, Miss.'

The plane roared into the grey clouds as Stella sat alone studying financial reports. At the far end of the plane, her two big bodyguards, Chester Draws and Chuck Brix, played a quiet game of cards.

But, hard as she tried, Stella was unable to concentrate on what she was reading. The printed words and figures kept floating away and she found herself thinking of the yellow cello leaning in the corner of her bedroom – the way it seemed to be looking at her.

And that strange smile...

CHAPTER THREE

Cellos Can't Walk

When Stella returned from Paris that evening, the yellow cello was still leaning in the corner of her bedroom.

'Aunt Zany!' she barked. 'Where are you?!'

Her aunt came staggering up the stairs, gasping and rattling.

'What's the matter?'

'That!'

Stella growled, pointing a fierce finger at the offending object. 'I told you to swap it for the parrot!'

'Please don't be angry, Stella. I tried to but I couldn't. The parrot was given to a little boy called Sandy Bottom and he doesn't want to swap it.'

'Why not? Why *not?!*'

She threw her hairbrush at the wall. It caught the dressing table, bounced back and hit Stella on the nose.

'Ow-ow-ow-ow-ow!'

She collapsed onto the bed, rubbing her throbbing hooter.

'Why won't he swap?'

'Because he's very happy with the parrot.'

'It's not *fair*,' Stella grumbled. 'The parrot should've been given to *me*. I'm the one who's come off worst in this deal.'

'It wasn't a deal, Stella. The cello was a generous gift.'

'How can it be generous when the person was dead?'

'Stella! That's a shocking thing to say!'

'Well, it's true. She couldn't play it any more, could she?'

'But it was very kind of her to think of you when she wrote her will.'

'Why are you creating such a fuss? It's not made of solid gold or anything. It's just an ordinary, boring old cello.'

'Some old instruments can produce wonderful music.'

Stella frowned and pouted.

'Anyhow, it's not valuable, because that was the first question I asked Mr Beeswax when he brought it here. I'm not stupid.'

'In that case,' said Aunt Zany with a weary sigh, 'why don't you give it away to a little boy or girl who wants a cello and can't afford to buy one? Wouldn't that be a nice thing to do?'

It was as if she had said, '*Why don't you stick your head in a bucket of wet cement and leave it there?*'

'Give it away?' Stella whispered.

Then she drew in a deep, deep breath.

'*Give it away?!*' she thundered. 'Nobody gets rich by giving things away! Have you taken leave of your pill-bewildered senses?'

Aunt Zany clutched her face in despair. 'It was only a suggestion,' she murmured.

Later, as Stella climbed into bed, she thought, 'I never want to clap eyes on that stupid yellow cello ever again!'

During the night, she dreamt the cello was dancing around the room, playing her a tune. She turned over in her sleep, but the music kept on singing in her head.

The next morning, Stella and her aunt were having breakfast together in the dining room. Stella was reading the newspaper. Aunt Zany was about to throw a handful of brown pills into her mouth when Stella exclaimed, 'Steaming stock brokers!'

Aunt Zany missed her mouth and the pills went flying out of the open window.

'Look! Here, in the Articles Wanted section, it says: *Needed urgently – a cello. Will pay £10.*'

Her aunt had a nasty idea what was coming.

'Quick, Aunt Zany, call this number and tell them they can have my cello for twenty pounds.'

A few minutes later, Aunt Zany was speaking to someone on the phone. She turned to Stella, putting her hand over the receiver. 'He says he'll pay you twelve pounds for it.'

'Is that all? Give it to me.' She tore the phone from her aunt. 'Hello, this is Stella Wishbone speaking. I'm the one who owns the cello and I can't afford to sell it for less than eighteen pounds. It's worth much more.'

'I tell ya what I need it for, Stella. My name's Paul Quickly.'

'I've heard of you. You're a famous rock singer!'

'Yeah, well – I'm the lead singer with Terrible Breath an' we do this number, innit, all about killin' an' violence, an' I smash me guitar ta bits. Just an old one, see? Well, we got this gig at Wembley tonight, right? An' I want one of the group to bring on a cello an' pretend to play a few notes, right? Give the number a bit of class. Then I grab the cello off 'im an' smash it ta bits. Innit? I put me foot through it and jump on it.

'The crowd goes mad. They love it. It's great. Then I set fire ta the piana and the drums blow up. An' that's the end of the number, see?'

'Yes, I see. It sounds very... loud.'

'Anyroad, I can't afford more than twelve quid. Gets a bit expensive smashin' up new instruments each time. 'Ow about thirteen?'

'Seventeen pounds,' Stella replied, 'and that's as low as I can go.'

'OK. Fourteen quid, then.'

'Sixteen pounds, and that's my last offer,' Stella said.

'Fifteen, and that's me absolute limit.'

'Done,' said Stella. 'It's all yours.'

And the yellow cello was sold.

And that is the end of the story. Or is it?

Or innit?

'Aunt Zany, I'm flying to New York in my pink plane this afternoon to buy a raincoat.'

'But you have hundreds of raincoats!'

'They're all boring. While I'm gone, will you please deliver the cello to that rock singer with Terrible Breath and collect the fifteen pounds from him?'

Aunt Zany said she would do as Stella asked – she didn't dare to do anything else.

When Stella returned the next day, she said, 'Did you sell the cello?'

'Yes, and I've left the cheque for fifteen pounds on your desk in the study.'

'Wonderful. Thank you, Aunt Zany. You are the best aunt in the whole world.'

And she gave her an affectionate hug and kiss.

Stella could charm the boots off a stone statue when it suited her. However, her sweet-tempered moods were few and far between and not very long-lasting.

'Did you buy yourself a lovely raincoat in New York?'

'No, they didn't have one I liked.'

Rich people can be very difficult to please.

Stella went off to her study, thinking, '*I'd better just make sure Mr Quickly signed and dated the cheque correctly.*'

Half way across the dark purple carpet she froze in her tracks. Leaning in the corner of her study was – the yellow cello.

'Aunt Zany! Come here *immediately!*'

There was a clattering noise from downstairs in the kitchen as dozens of pills bounced and skittered across the marble floor. A few moments later, Aunt Zany peered fearfully through the study door.

'What's the matter?'

'Are you playing some sort of a joke on me?'

Aunt Zany's eyes widened with anxiety. 'What do you mean?'

'You did *not* sell the cello!'

'I did.'

'It's still here!'

'Where?'

'There!' Stella gestured dramatically with both hands.

'Aaah!' Aunt Zany exclaimed weakly. 'It can't be. It's impossible. I took it to Mr Quickly's house in Cricklewood and he gave me the cheque for fifteen pounds. Then I came straight home and put the cheque on your desk, right – '

She was about to say 'here' when she saw that the cheque was neither here nor there. Nor anywhere else in the room.

'Where has it gone? I don't understand.'

'How many pills have you swallowed today?'

'I'm telling you the truth. I sold the cello. I did.'

'What's it doing here, then?'

19

'I don't know. Oh I can't cope. I just can't cope.'

Stella was about to reply but the front doorbell rang.

'That may be your new secretary, Stella. I'll go and see,' her Aunt suggested, eager to escape.

Stella picked up the telephone and called the rock singer.

'Is that Paul Quickly?'

'Yeah. Who's this?'

'Stella Wishbone. Your cello is here.'

'Did you nick it out of my van? What are you like?!'

Before she could say any more, he carried on.

'Look, Stella, I don't like bein' messed about. It ain't cool. If you didn't really wanna sell that cello, why didn't ya say so in the first place?'

'But I *did* want to sell it. I *do!*'

'Well, you've got a funny way of showin' it. What I can't work out, is 'ow you got inside my van. It was padlocked.'

'What are you talking about? I've just flown back from New York.'

'Look, your aunt, she brings the cello over 'ere, right? Nice lady, Miss 'Andlebar, but a funny sort of customer. Does she make a rattlin' noise when she dodges about? Thought summink was goin' wrong with my ears. Innit.'

'Yes she does. It's her lucky Mexican beads. Go on.'

'I give 'er the cheque, right? And she 'ands over the cello, which I lock up in the back of me van. So, couple of hours later, we was drivin' down to Wembley for the gig, innit? When we gets there, I opens up the van – no cello! Its gone. And there's the cheque, pokin' out of one of me loudspeakers. I mean, do me a favour.'

'Mr Quickly, there's obviously been a ridiculous mix up. My aunt will bring the cello over to you immediately. Give her the cheque again and – '

'Nah, too late now. I did the number last night. I smashed up a flute instead. Well, snapped it in 'alf, really. The crowd didn't scream very loud. Don't fink most of 'em could see what I done. Anyroad, no 'ard feelin's. But next time you do business, make ya mind up. Right? See ya.'

And he rang off.

'What on earth is going on?' Stella wondered. 'Cellos can't walk through locked doors. Or even *un*-locked doors!'

She glanced at the cello.

It seemed to be gazing innocently up at the ceiling, as if to say, *'Don't look at me. I had absolutely nothing to do with it.'*

Or was it Stella's imagination?

'What I need is a really efficient secretary to sort these things out for me. Is that asking too much, for goodness' sake?'

Aunt Zany appeared in the doorway.

'Your new secretary has arrived.'

She gave a nervous smile.

'Good,' Stella replied. 'Maybe I'll have better luck with this one. What's her name?'

And in he strolled.

CHAPTER FOUR

Call Me Stella

'Hello. My name is Steele. Stirling Steele.'

Stella gazed up into his face, unable to speak. He was the most handsome man she had ever seen. He reminded her of an Olympic Games athlete in his white summer jacket and grey slacks, with his thick, fair hair and his sparkling blue eyes, and his charming smile.

'It's *really amazing* to meet you, Miss Wishbone. I've heard so much about you.'

They shook hands.

'Knockout place you've got here. I'm well impressed.'

'Are you sure you want to be a secretary?' she asked.

Mr Steele looked puzzled. 'Of course. Why?'

'Wouldn't you rather be a film star?'

'Me? Oh no. I'd feel really embarrassed with everybody staring at me. I'm a very private person. Almost shy.'

'You could be a famous pop singer. Or a man who wears knitted cardigans in magazines and looks pleased about something,' Stella insisted.

'Do you really think so? Really? It's very kind of you to say that, Miss Wishbone.' And his smile got wider and wider, revealing rows of dazzling teeth, whiter than royal dinner plates.

'What beautiful teeth you have!' she gasped.

'All the better to eat you with, as the Wolf said to Snow White.'

And he laughed, revealing even more flawless nibblers and gnashers.

'I've got crooked teeth,' said Stella. 'In the front. Look.'

She opened her mouth and pointed to her front lower teeth which were, indeed, a bit uneven.

'Shall we get on with the interview?' Aunt Zany suggested anxiously. 'Please take a seat, Mr Steele.'

They all sat down.

'In your application letter here,' Aunt Zany continued, 'you say you can swim, dive, do cartwheels, walk on your hands up and down stairs, play jacks, charades, monopoly, ping-pong, crack your big toes and do gorilla impressions. Do you think these skills would come in useful as a secretary?'

'They might,' he replied with engaging optimism. 'Life's full of surprises.'

'You're quite right. It is,' Stella agreed, nodding her head vigorously.

'It also says that you went to school at Rugby, where you won "First Prize".'

'I did.'

'What for?'

'Rugby.'

'It's a ball game for aristocrats,' Stella explained. 'I'm well impressed.'

Aunt Zany looked slightly pained by the phrase.

'Tell me, Mr Steele,' she continued, 'do you take short-hand?'

'Actually... ' He flicked his golden hair from his forehead. 'I don't. No.'

'Can you type?' she asked.

He crossed his legs, smiling. 'Not very well. No.'

'Can you use a computer?'

'Let me see... ' He scratched his ear. 'No.'

'Or a fax machine?'

He rubbed his nose. 'I never actually, erm – no.'

'Do you know anything about data filing?'

He adjusted his neatly knotted tie. 'Not really, no.'

'Financial accounts?'

'No.'

'Commercial contracts?'

'No.'

'Tax laws?'

'No.'

'Business management?'

'No.'

'Do you speak any foreign languages?'

'No.'

'Do you have any previous secretarial experience or references at all, Mr Steele?'

He folded his arms and cleared his throat. 'Well, there was, er – no.'

'I see,' said Aunt Zany, not overly impressed. 'In that case – '

'In that case,' Stella interrupted, 'the job's yours. I'll pay you double the normal wages, if that's acceptable.'

'Wow!' Mr Steele exclaimed.

Stella stood up. 'Would you like some ice-cream?'

'You betcha!'

Aunt Zany looked highly alarmed. 'Don't you want to ask Mr Steele any questions, Stella?'

Stella considered for a moment.

'Chocolate, banana or raspberry flavour?' she enquired.

'Chocolate, please,' he answered eagerly. 'You mean I've got the job? *Really*?'

'Yes, you have,' said Stella before Aunt Zany could protest. 'Can you start today?'

'Sure. That's really *great!*'

Aunt Zany's frown deepened. 'But Stella, what about – ?'

'You remind me of my father,' Stella went on, her voice trembling slightly with emotion.

'Do I? Well, I take that as an absolutely brilliant compliment, Miss Wishbone,' he replied with quiet sincerity. 'I really do.'

Considering that Stella's father had been a small, tubby, bald-headed, podgy-faced man, you might suspect that her sense of judgement was slightly off balance.

'Yes, it's something about your smile,' she added wistfully.

Her father, if you remember, never smiled because he had no sense of humour at all.

'What's your lucky number?' Stella asked.

'Often.'

'Often isn't a number,' Aunt Zany pointed out.

'But if I enjoy doing something, like playing football, I'm lucky if I do it often.'

'Excellent answer,' Stella announced. 'What's your favourite insect?'

'That would be... ' He spoke as if trying to make a guess. 'A butterfly?'

'Incredible! That's my favourite as well!'

Aunt Zany sighed.

'Stella, your favourite insect is a scorpion. You keep one in your bedroom. She's called Sarah Nade.'

'Who is your favourite historical character?'

'Robin Hood. That guy's one super-cool dude.'

'Stella, he stole from the rich and gave to the poor,' Aunt Zany warned her.

Mr Steele cut in quickly. 'Oh, I don't take any notice of that boring stuff. I just like the green outfit and the way he rides through the forest singing songs and shooting people with a bow and arrow.'

'I've never heard of Robin Hood,' Stella said. 'Was he like a Green protester who lives up a tree?'

'He was the first, you might say, yeah.'

His smile vanished as he put on a serious face.

'Although he was an action hero, I think, deep down, he was painfully shy and humble. And *really* sincere. I *really* admire those qualities in a person.'

'Perhaps because you're like that too,' Stella suggested.

He lowered his eyes, modestly.

'I do try.'

'I forgot something,' Stella announced, sitting down again. 'Do you have any questions to ask *me*?'

'Just one, maybe.' He gave her an innocent smile. 'Do your father and mother live here with you?'

'No. Both my parents are dead.'

'That is *really* sad,' he said sympathetically, wiping away an invisible tear. 'So are mine.'

'How terrific!' Stella exclaimed.

Her aunt was appalled. 'Stella!'

'I mean because we've got tons of things in common.'

'We have!' Mr Steele agreed, equally impressed. 'It's like – incredible! And please, all my special friends call me Stir.'

'Stir?' Aunt Zany repeated. 'Isn't that a slang word for prison?'

'Yeah! Have you spent time inside as well?' He hurriedly corrected himself. 'I mean – have you spent time inside libraries studying the origins of colourful English phrases?'

Stella stood up.

'It's short for Stirling, Aunt Zany.'

She turned to Mr Steele and pulled a *she's-so-stupid* face.

'Come with me down to the kitchen. I'll show you where the fridge is, so you can help yourself to ice cream or fruit juice any time you want.'

'Fantastic!' said Mr Steele, following Stella out of the room.

He flashed a film star smile over his shoulder at Aunt Zany.

'It was *really* nice to meet you, Miss Handlebar. Catch you later.'

Aunt Zany gave him a polite nod.

She was thinking, '*Really* nice, *really* great, *really* terrific. I wonder what he's *really* up to. I smell trouble. Oh dear, I can't cope. I just can't cope.'

As they tucked into chocolate ice cream, Mr Steele said, 'I don't think Miss Handlebar considers me cut out for the job.'

'Doesn't matter. I do.'

'Great. So tell me, your aunt, is she the only family you've got?'

'Yes, worse luck.'

'No other relatives looking after you in this house?'

'No, just her.'

'I see!' He nodded his head sympathetically, as if the news came as a huge surprise. 'Yeah, I get the picture.'

'She's alright, I suppose. But she can be a bit of a pain.'

'It's odd. When I first shook hands with her, I heard a sort of rattling noise, like someone was tapping on the window.'

'It's her pills. She takes about five hundred a day. You'll get used to it.'

Mr Steele looked at her with wide-eyed curiosity.

'Is she ill?'

'No but she thinks she is.'

'So what are all those pills for?'

'Everything. She keeps them on these shelves.'

Stella opened a cupboard next to the fridge. It was stacked with boxes and bottles containing pills of every shape and colour. A list of instructions was pinned to the inside of the cupboard door.

'Look,' said Stella. 'She stuck this note here to remind her what they're all for.'

She read the list aloud.

> '*MY BROWN PILLS:*
> *These are to stop me Ranting and Raving,*
> *Moaning, Groaning, Panting and Craving.*
> *MY YELLOW PILLS:*
> *These are to stop me Croaking and Muttering,*
> *Wheezing, Sneezing, Choking and Stuttering.*
> *MY WHITE PILLS:*
> *And these are to stop me Fumbling and Fiddling,*
> *Slipping, Tripping, Mumbling and Pidd –* '

Stella broke off, looking a little sheepish.

'Sorry, the last word is a bit personal.'

'What are the others for?' Mr Steele asked, fascinated.

> '*MY BLUE PILLS:*
> *These are to stop me Flushing and Steaming,*
> *Cramping, Stamping, Blushing and Beaming.*
> *MY GREEN PILLS:*
> *These are to stop me Stinking and Whiffing,*
> *Slurping, Burping, Blinking and Sniffing.*
> *MY ORANGE PILLS:*
> *And these are to stop me Stopping and Starting,*
> *Wailing, Flailing, Flopping and Far –* '

She hesitated again.

'I shouldn't mention the last one either,' Stella commented, grinning.

'Her stomach must be like a chemical factory,' Mr Steele

observed, gazing at the pills, his blue eyes glittering with interest. He ate another spoonful of ice-cream thoughtfully.

'What would happen to her if somebody took – I mean, if she suddenly stopped taking the pills?'

'She'd probably explode.'

'Like a nuclear chain reaction?'

'Something like that.'

They both laughed at the idea.

'Or,' he suggested, 'she might fly around the room like a balloon when you blow it up and then let go of it.'

'She would,' Stella agreed, nodding and grinning.

He stared strangely at the far distance.

'And then she'd fall to the floor with nothing inside her, limp and lifeless.'

For a moment, he appeared gleefully mesmerised by the vision of Aunt Zany's horrible fate.

'How is your ice-cream, Mr Steele?'

'Really great, thanks.' He took another mouthful.

'You made an excellent impression on me right from the start,' Stella said.

'Did I? Really?'

He sounded *really* happy.

'Yes, because you didn't look at my cello and say, '*Oh, what an unusual cello. It's yellow!*' I hate people who say that. As if I didn't already *know* it was yellow!'

'Is it a *real* cello? I thought it was one of those genuine fake antique jobbies with concealed doors that you open and there's a TV set inside.'

'I wish. That would be far more useful. But I'm going to swap it for a parrot tomorrow. More ice-cream, Mr – I mean, Stir?'

'Yes, please, Miss Wishbone.'

'Same flavour?'

'How about raspberry this time? My favourite'

'That's my favourite too! Oh, by the way, before we start work, there's just one more thing I have to say.'

He froze.

'Oh? What's that?'

He sounded nervous, as if bracing himself for a tricky question that might spoil everything.

'If I'm going to call you Stir, you've got to call me Stella.'

His fears vanished instantly and he smiled with delight.

'Oh I see! Can I really call you Stella? Wow! What an honour! Thank you – Stella.'

His job interview had gone better than he had dared to hope. No tricky questions.

Mr Steele was well pleased.

CHAPTER FIVE

The Monster

'You're supposed to do what I tell you!'

Stella was having a blazing row with her ninety year old gardener, Phil Waterbutts – a bent, wrinkled, weather-beaten little man, with only one eye and deaf as a dock leaf.

'Eh? What did you say?'

'I said,' Stella shouted into his hearing-aid, 'I want roses down the drive, marigolds round the pond and asters up the front steps!'

'What? Last week you wanted lupins down the drive, pansies round the pond and tulips up the front steps. Have you got ants in your pants or something? This is a garden, not a shop window in Oxford Street.'

'I know it's a garden. It's *my* garden. It belongs to *me*. And I pay you to look after it, so you'll do as I say.'

'Oh will I?'

Phil Waterbutts screwed his face up like a pickled walnut.

'Well, I'll tell you what I am. I'm a gardener, not a push-button machine! And I don't like having orders fired at me every five minutes by a little squit like you.'

Stella stared at him in open-mouthed outrage.

'What's more, these flowers are plants. They're not plastic. I can't keep digging them up one place and sticking them back another. They get dizzy.'

'I don't care if they get hiccups! I want different flowers in different places *every week* from now on.'

'Your father was bad enough – the miserable old maggot – but at least he left me alone to get on with my work.'

'How dare you call my father a maggot!'

'You're worse. You're a little monster.'

'How dare you call me a monster!'

''Cos that's what you are. A monster and a brat.'

'You're fired! Can you hear me?'

'Oh no I'm not,' he replied with a cackling laugh.

'You are! You're fired! YOU – ARE – *FIRED!*'

'Ha ha! You can't fire me, 'cos I gave my notice in to your aunt five minutes ago. I've been invited to live with my daughter and son-in-law in Mold. So you can plant your pansies where the sun don't shine!'

And with that, he switched off his hearing-aid and hobbled away.

'And good riddance!' Stella shouted after him.

Stella stormed into the kitchen, where Aunt Zany was washing down fifteen pills with a mouthful of tea.

'Where is Stir?!' she shouted.

Aunt Zany's eyes nearly popped out of her head. She staggered against the wall, thumped herself on the chest and the pills went down with a clatter, clunk, splosh.

'What is Stir?' Aunt Zany asked, looking alarmed. 'A foreign country?'

'No. My new secretary. That's what his special friends call him. He told us. Don't you remember?'

'Ah yes, Mr Steele. He hasn't arrived for work yet. In fact, he's over an hour late.'

Her tone of disapproval was ignored by Stella.

'It's probably not his fault.'

'You made friends with him very quickly.'

'I think he's marvellous. I feel I can really trust him.'

'Why is that, Stella?'

'Because he's handsome and he's got a pleasant smile and he's really nice to me.'

'I don't quite follow your logic. Remember the old saying. *"You can't always judge a book by its cover."'*

'He's not a book. He's a person.'

'People have insides just like books, and I don't mean their lungs and livers. I mean what makes them tick.'

'Now you're talking as if he were a clock.'

'And there's another old saying, Stella. *"Handsome is as handsome does."'*

'Does what?'

'It's not so much what people *look* like as how they *behave* that matters.'

Just then, Mr Steele appeared.

'Morning all,' he said in a charmingly breezy manner.

Aunt Zany was not charmed.

'Mr Steele. You are an hour late.'

He smiled at Stella. 'Have I missed something?'

'Not really,' she replied, totally charmed. 'I just sacked Waterbutts, the gardener. I'll need a new one. Would you see to that, Aunt Zany? Oh, and tell Rex Bollards, my driver, that I'll need the car at two o'clock.' She smiled at Stir and added confidentially, 'I'm going to see a boy about a parrot.'

'That sounds really exciting. Can I come with you?'

'You're supposed to stay here and take my phone calls.'

'It would be much more fun to go for a drive with you and see a parrot. Is it a real one or stuffed?'

Aunt Zany frowned. 'Mr Steele, we hope you find working here pleasant, even enjoyable, but you can't always expect it to be fun. It is work, after all, and sometimes quite hard work.'

Stella scowled, dangerously.

'Aunt Zany, I asked you to see about the car and to find a new gardener.'

'But Stella, I'm not your secretary. Mr Steele is.'

'I want a private word with him, if you don't mind.'

Aunt Zany's lower lip trembled and tears filled her sad eyes as she rattled out of the kitchen.

'The gardener just said I was a monster. Do you think I am?'

'Oh no! How could anyone say that? I think you're terrific.'

'Do you *really?*'

There wasn't a shred of doubt in her mind; she just wanted to hear him say it again.

'Oh yes. I think you're clever, attractive, friendly, amusing, intelligent, talented, imaginative, fascinating, delightful, witty, helpful, charming, thoughtful, sympathetic, generous and *really* fabulous company. And I'm not just saying that to flatter you.'

'Shall we get married?' she asked.

'You're a bit too young at the moment, Stella, but it's really kind of you to ask. I'm afraid you'll have to wait about ten more years before you can marry someone. I'll be over thir– I mean, I'll be almost thirty by then.'

'Thirty!' she gasped. 'Oh no. That's horribly old.'

'Never mind. We can still be friends.'

'I hate being small. Everyone treats you like a child. Do you know what else Waterbutts called me? A squit.'

'He's obviously very stupid. I'm not a snob, but I think poor people who have to do horrible jobs can be very spiteful sometimes.'

'So you don't think I'm a – what he said?'

'Honestly, I really and truly think you're incredibly fantastic. Mark you, I would say one thing, though.'

'What?' Stella asked anxiously.

'I hope you don't mind me mentioning it, but I get the feeling that you aren't totally happy.'

'You're right. I'm not. How can you tell?'

'Oh, little things. Like the way you sometimes go red in the face and scream and wave your fists about and smash plates and rip up newspapers. Small things other people might not notice, but I do. Would you like my advice, Stella? – for what it's worth,' he added modestly.

'Yes, I would.'

'I think you need a lot more money. I think it's as simple as that. I really do.'

'More money... ' Stella repeated, thoughtfully.

'If you had twice as much money as you've got now, I'm convinced you'd be twice as happy.'

'That sounds like good sense,' she said, nodding sagely. 'But the thing is, I've got quite a lot of money already.'

Considering she was the wealthiest little girl in the entire world, she expressed herself very lightly on the subject.

'Yeah, but the amazing thing about money,' Mr Steele explained, 'is that you can never have enough. I've met stacks of really rich people and none of them seemed pleased with the amount of money they had. Look, while you're swapping the cello, I'll see if I can work out an idea. I can't promise anything definite at this stage, but I might be able to help.'

He gave Stella the impression that somewhere behind his sparkling blue eyes, an ingenious plan was already forming itself – something brilliant and tremendously exciting.

In a voice like butter and honey dripping from hot toast, he said, 'Leave it with me, Stella. The most important thing is that you should be happy. And you will be. I really mean that. Trust me.'

'Thank you,' she said in a spellbound whisper. 'I do trust you. Really.'

CHAPTER SIX

Sandy Bottom

PING was snapped up the moment Stella's FOR SALE advert appeared in the newspaper.

It had attracted the interest of several people, most particularly Robin Banks – a rich property developer. Or, as Stella put it, a sleazy crook.

He specialised in buying beautiful old houses, tearing them down and sticking up ugly, cheaply made 'luxury flats', and selling them at a vast profit, thus making himself very pleased and everyone who lived nearby very angry. To him, the Peckham Institute for the Nervous and Gifted was just another juicy kill.

'PING looks perfect,' he had thought. And pounced!

'That's it,' Stella said, putting down her pen. 'Signed, sealed and sold.'

'What is?' asked Aunt Zany.

'PING. Robin Banks has bought it for a tidy sum,' she replied, putting on her coat.

'Oh no!' wailed Aunt Zany. 'Not that horrible Banks man. You've had dealings with him before. He's a heartless money-grabber. He'll throw the children onto the streets and bulldoze their school into the ground!'

'As far as I'm concerned, he can do whatever he likes. It's his now,' she said, grabbing her briefcase.

'It's wicked,' Aunt Zany whispered, deeply upset.

'It's business,' Stella answered firmly. 'Right, see you later. I'm off to swap that yellow cello for a parrot.'

'Oh no, Stella. Please don't get rid of your cello. I beg you.'

Stella trotted down the stairs and out of the front door to her waiting car. Aunt Zany sped after her. Rattle-rattle.

'The cello was a special gift. You should keep it.'

'Why should I?' Stella asked, irritably. 'Do stop making such a fuss.'

'Can't you, er – save it for a rainy day?' suggested her aunt, trying desperately to appeal to Stella's sense of greed.

'Save it? It isn't money, Aunt Zany. A fat lot of use a yellow cello would be on a rainy day.'

And she jumped into the back seat of her car.

'Bollards! Did you put the cello in the boot?'

'Yes, miss.'

'Right. Let's go!'

The long, sleek limousine moved smoothly off, leaving Aunt Zany at the front door looking even more woebegone than usual.

'Stella's going from bad to worse. Where will it end? I can't cope. I just can't cope.'

'What a dismal looking place,' Stella announced, as her car pulled up in front of an isolated cottage near Slough.

The building was, indeed, in a sad state – cracked chimney pots, missing slates, crumbling brickwork, rotten window frames, damp stains where the gutters leaked, peeling paintwork – everything needed seeing to.

Instead of a number, the cottage had a name:

HAPPY DAYS

'They ought to call it Better Days, because that's what this house has seen.'

The hinges on the front gate were broken so Stella had to lift and push to open it. She then picked her way carefully down the weed-choked path, carrying her briefcase.

'People don't deserve to have a house if they can't look after it properly.'

BELL NOT WORKING

– said a scribbled note pinned to the front door. She thumped on it with her fist.

Bang, bang, bang!

There was a long silence.

She was about to thump again when the door was pulled open a few inches by a frowning, pinch-faced woman.

'Yes, what do you want?' She sounded impatient, as if Stella was already making a nuisance of herself.

'Does Sandy Bottom live here?'

'Why do you ask?'

'I've come to speak to him.'

'What about?' the woman asked sharply.

'I want to swap his parrot for a yellow cello.'

'Is this some kind of practical joke?'

'My aunt rang you about it last week.'

'I haven't the faintest idea what you're babbling about. Sandy is not interested in swapping his parrot for anything, so please stop bothering him and go away.'

'Listen. I paid a private eye a lot of money to track down this address and I insist on speaking to Sandy Bottom *personally*.'

'Well you can't. So kindly go away and leave us alone.'

And she shut the door abruptly in Stella's face.

Stella banged again. The door opened two seconds later.

'My name is Stella Wish – '

'Didn't you hear what I said, little girl? Go away!' the woman repeated, glaring down at Stella angrily.

Stella glared back. 'My name is Stella Wishbone and I'm very rich and no one shuts the door on me. I've driven all the way from London specially to talk to Sandy Bottom. And I'm going to. So there! And I'm *very rich!*'

'Who is it, mum?' came a young voice from inside the house.

'Just a moment, Sandy,' the woman called over her shoulder. When she turned to face Stella again, she looked quite different – almost pleasant.

'Wishbone? Did you say your name was Stella Wishbone?'

'Yes. And I'm very rich,' she replied to make her position absolutely clear.

Mrs Bottom's expression softened even more.

'I've heard about you.'

'From the newspapers, probably. I'm famous.'

'Your father died last year.'

'Yes he did. I'm also very rich,' she repeated, just in case the message hadn't got home.

'Forgive me, Stella, I didn't realise who you were. I'm so sorry about your father. Of course you can come in and talk to Sandy, but I must explain something,' she said, lowering her voice. 'Sandy is not well. He mustn't be upset, so please don't ask him to give you his parrot. He's very fond of it.'

Sandy's mother didn't look at all angry now, just worried and extremely tired.

Stella followed her into the dark hall which smelt damp and mouldy.

'Sandy can't manage the stairs anymore, so I've moved his bed down here to the front room. It saves my legs as well.'

Mrs Bottom was about to open the door when she paused and said something that puzzled Stella.

'You're exactly the same age as Sandy.'

'How do you know?'

For a few silent moments, Mrs Bottom gazed at Stella with a look of great sadness. Without replying, she opened the door of the small front room.

'Sandy, you've got a visitor from London! Her name is Stella,' she explained, trying to make the news sound jolly.

'Stella, this is my son, Sandy.'

He was sitting up in bed reading a book.

'Hello,' he said eagerly, taking off his spectacles. 'Sorry for not getting up.' With a bright smile, he leaned forward to shake hands with her.

Stella was shocked to discover how small and thin Sandy was, especially if they really were the same age. He appeared to be almost half her size.

She also noticed a wheelchair next to his bed.

'Why have you come all the way from London to see me?' Sandy asked.

'Because of your parrot,' she began. 'I was wondering if you would – '

'Stella was wondering if you would let her have a look at him,' his mother interrupted. 'Somebody told her how handsome Batty is and she wanted to see for herself. Isn't that right, Stella?'

Stella muttered, 'Yes, that's right,' and pouted sulkily.

'*Silly idiot! Stupid fool!*' another voice cried out, giving Stella quite a start.

It sounded like a woman. Stella turned round angrily, assuming the words were aimed at her.

And there was the parrot.

He was sitting on a tall wooden perch by the window. He leaned his head to one side and fixed Stella with a round, black, beady eye.

The second shock for Stella was the bird's appearance. Handsome was the word. His feathers were a soft, pale grey, except for his head which was almost white, and his tail – a slash of vivid red.

'This is my parrot,' Sandy announced proudly. 'His name is Batty.'

CHAPTER SEVEN

Batty and Dottie

'*Stupid fool!*' cried the parrot.

'What an unfriendly bird,' said Stella.

'I don't think he means it. He's picked it up somewhere. He says lots of different things.'

As if to prove Sandy's point, Batty called out, '*Fares, please! Hold very tight!*'

Something about the parrot's voice puzzled Stella. It sounded oddly familiar but for the moment she couldn't work out why.

'He's very tame, so he must like people. Do you want him to sit on your shoulder?'

'I don't know,' said Stella nervously. 'Does he bite?'

'He hasn't so far. Go on – put your finger in front of his toes and he'll walk up your arm.' Stella did as Sandy suggested, half fascinated and half afraid.

The parrot looked down at Stella's hand and then stepped calmly onto her finger and made its way up her arm, as if going for a leisurely stroll.

Stella was glad she was wearing her coat. The claws didn't hurt at all but they made her feel a bit peculiar.

Mrs Bottom tilted the fireplace mirror so that Stella could see herself with Batty perched on her shoulder. The extraordinary sight made Stella smile.

Sandy laughed. 'You look like an old sea dog, marooned on a desert island with buried treasure.'

'Why is he called Batty?' she asked.

'We don't know. He's an African Grey. The Latin name is interesting – Psitacus Erithacus. Do you know what it means? Unknown Bird. King Henry VIII had one exactly like Batty at

Hampton Court. When the king wanted to get across the River Thames, his parrot whistled for a boatman to ferry them over.'

'Handy,' Stella remarked.

'And when the boatman had rowed King Henry to the other side, the parrot said, "*Give me a groat*." So the story goes.'

'Belonging to that king, it's a wonder it didn't say, "*Off with his head*,"' she commented, wryly.

Sandy and his mother laughed.

'Were you surprised when you got him?' Stella asked, feeling very jealous.

'Yes. It was odd. Last week, a man called Mr Beeswax turned up here carrying a birdcage with Batty inside.'

'A stupid solicitor. You're lucky he didn't drop the cage.'

'He said, 'A lady has died and left a will. And in the will she wrote, "*I want Sandy Bottom to look after my parrot, Batty.*" Then Mr Beeswax said, "*So Batty is yours now. Forthwith.*"'

Stella could barely contain her boiling resentment.

'He told me this lady found out I was under the weather and that I like birds. She thought Batty would be good company for me. She even put it in her will. "*Batty will talk to Master Bottom and cheer him up.*" It's the best present I ever had.'

'She left me a cello. It doesn't say anything.'

'Sandy, tell her the story about how Batty was born,' his mother prompted, tidying up.

'According to Mr Beeswax, a long time ago in Africa, there were two little girls who found an egg that had fallen out of a tree. They kept it warm and hatched it, and out came a parrot. When they grew up, one of the sisters took the parrot with her to England to live in a lighthouse.'

'Olive Underfelt. She was a distant relative of mine.'

Batty let out an ear-shattering whistle and shrugged his shoulders.

'How old is Batty?' Stella asked.

'Mr Beeswax said he's thirty-five.'

The two young people gazed at the ancient parrot in awed silence, wondering what he had seen and what he knew.

'I don't approve of making pets of wild animals,' Sandy continued, 'especially keeping them in cages – unless they're sick or need protection. I think they should be allowed to live naturally. But once you've tamed a wild creature, it relies on you and forgets how to search for food, so you have to take care of it. That's what's happened to Batty. He's completely tame. We even take him out for walks. He flies around, but he never flies away. Do you like donkeys?'

'Donkeys?' Stella was a bit surprised by the question. 'I don't know any.'

'Would you like to meet one? She lives in a field behind a pub. I go and visit her nearly every day. And Batty comes too.'

'I own a stable of thoroughbred racehorses,' she replied flatly. 'I breed them and sell them.'

'Oh.' Sandy said, and blinked at her, feeling somewhat deflated. 'Right.'

'I didn't come all this way from London to look at a donkey. I came here to – '

Sandy's mother caught her eye.

'Oh well, OK then. Where is it?'

'Mum, can I take Stella to meet Dottie?'

A few minutes later, Stella was pushing Sandy in his wheelchair along the lane, with Batty perched on her shoulder.

It was quite hard work for Stella and she was soon in a muck sweat.

'Do you ever go bird-watching?' Sandy asked her.

'No. I'm too busy making money,' she replied testily.

'Bird-watching was my favourite hobby before I was ill. I think birds are amazing creatures. Imagine what it must be like to fly.'

'I fly all the time. I've got two private jet planes.'

'No, I don't mean inside a metal tube. I mean really fly – jump into space and go zooming through the air and land on the top of a tree or a chimney pot. It must be wonderful. I want to create a bird sanctuary when I'm older. What do you want to do when you grow up?'

'I don't know. Be the richest person in the whole world, I suppose.'

'I thought you were already rich.'

'I'm only the richest *girl* in the world at the moment,' she said casually, making it sound a pretty humdrum state of affairs.

The sun was shining and by the time they reached the field Stella was out of breath.

Batty flew to the fence and said, '*Silly idiot. Stupid fool.*'

'Yes, I am a silly idiot,' Stella thought, 'to be wasting my valuable time like this.'

Sandy greeted the donkey like a dear old friend.

'Hello Dottie, how are you today? You're looking well.'

Dottie seemed very pleased to see her visitors, especially when they collected handfuls of thick, juicy grass and fed it to her through the fence. She munched the grass noisily.

'This is Stella. She's come all the way from London. That's a big city where lots of clever people live. You're clever too, aren't you, Dottie? Of course you are. You can eat grass. We can't.'

Stella frowned. 'Why are you talking to this donkey? It doesn't understand what you're saying.'

'She likes it. Don't you, Dottie?'

'That's silly. It's a dumb animal. It can't reply.'

'Dottie's got a mind of her own, make no mistake. She's a real character, and she loves company.'

'It's just a donkey.'

Dottie gazed at Stella with large, watchful eyes and took another mouthful of grass from Stella's hand.

'Ow! She nipped my finger.'

'There you are,' Sandy said, grinning. 'Maybe she understands more than you imagine. In her own way.'

This gave Stella something to think about.

'What sort of illness have you got?' she asked.

'A rare blood disease. The doctors don't know how to cure it.'

'Is it serious?'

'Yes. I get very tired and can't walk far. I have to be taken to hospital for fresh blood three times a week. It's awful for my mother because she's had to give up her teaching job to look after me and we haven't got much money. I hear her crying sometimes.'

'Haven't you got a father?'

'No. He was a plumber. One day he went off to mend someone's sink and never came back. Mum says he ran away with another lady.'

Stella suddenly understood why Happy Days was in such a shabby, run-down state, and why Sandy's mother looked so worried and tired.

'Are you going to die?' she asked solemnly.

'I might.'

'Are you scared?'

'Not really. I should think it'll be quite interesting. A bit like going to the moon.'

'You're just pretending to be brave. If I thought I was going to die, I'd be really frightened.'

'But you *are* going to die,' he said simply. 'Everybody is.'

'Not for years and years. And by then I'll be so old I won't care.'

'How do you know? It might be tonight. Anything could happen.'

Dottie the donkey was looking deeply into Stella's eyes as she munched her grass, as if to say, 'Well?'

Stella was lost for a reply. This had given her something else to think about.

'All I can say,' she declared finally, 'is that you seem remarkably cheerful, in spite of all your problems.'

'Thank you,' Sandy replied, smiling. 'I suppose I am, most of the time. I try to be for Mum. What about you? Have you got a mum and dad?'

'My mother died when I was very small – I can't even remember her. And my father died last year.'

'What a shame. Do you miss your dad?'

'Can't say I do. He was away most of the time, working or travelling.'

'Don't you have anyone to look after you at all?' Sandy asked in amazement.

'Of course I do, hundreds of people,' she replied haughtily. 'A housekeeper, maids, butlers, drivers, bodyguards, tutors, pilots, cooks. *And* a brilliant personal secretary!'

'But anyone special?'

'I've got an aunt. She pretends to look after me, but most of the time I look after *her*.'

'What about neighbours?'

'I never speak to them.'

'I suppose you've got lots of chums of your own age.'

'What for?'

'To play games with.'

'I don't play games. I market them.'

'Friends to visit?'

'I never visit people. I employ them.'

'To share jokes with?'

'I don't share jokes. I sell them.'

'Just to keep you company, then.'

'I've no time for company. I'm too busy.'

'Well,' said Sandy, looking utterly astonished, 'I think you're remarkably cheerful *too*, in spite of all *your* problems!'

And that gave Stella yet another thing to think about.

CHAPTER EIGHT

A Dream Donkey

'You're in luck. Look.'

Sandy handed his field binoculars to Stella and pointed.

'It's a green woodpecker.' He whispered, so as not to alarm the bird. 'On the dirt path over there.'

The large green and yellow bird with its crimson capped head was squatting in the dust and stretching its wings.

'What is he doing? '

'He's anting.'

'He's what?'

'He's found a group of ants and he's sitting on them.'

'What on earth for?'

'No one knows exactly. It may be a way of cleaning his feathers. Can you see? He's picking up ants and wiping them on himself.'

'How can ants clean his feathers?'

'Because when ants are attacked – or sat on – they spray formic acid. It's an insecticide, and it kills the feather lice.'

'Well I never,' she murmured.

Stella was hooked.

In the space of half an hour, the binoculars gave her wonderfully clear views of woodpigeons, blackbirds, house martins and jays. And one tiny wren – Stella's favourite.

By the time Stella had wheeled Sandy back to Happy Days, Mrs Bottom had prepared them a simple but delicious spread – a pot of tea, home-made bread and strawberry jam, chocolate cake and ginger biscuits.

Sandy had no appetite at all but Stella tucked in with great gusto. As she devoured her second piece of cake, she looked at Sandy. He seemed to be getting thinner and yet more cheerful by the second. He was positively bubbling over with interesting information about his favourite hobby.

'Mr Catch, the old groundsman at Iver Cross Cricket Club, said there's a local name for the green woodpecker. They call it the yaffingale.'

'What a funny word!' Stella exclaimed.

However, she had forgotten that her mouth was full of cake, so her remark sounded more like, 'Wob a fubby werp!' and a crumb shot out of her mouth and landed in Sandy's cup of tea – kerplop!

This struck Sandy as so funny, he couldn't speak for laughing, and the more Stella tried to behave properly, the more she couldn't *eat* for laughing, and for the next five minutes they were both helplessly gasping and spluttering and shaking with laughter.

In the kitchen, Mrs Bottom smiled to herself, pleased that they seemed to be getting along so well.

When they had both finally calmed down again, Sandy returned to his favourite subject.

'Little birds spend most of their time looking for food. Their bodies use up energy faster than big birds. A tiny goldcrest can eat a third of its weight a day!'

'All I can say about birds,' Stella said, 'is that when I was in Hong Kong on business, I ate bird's nest soup.'

'Oh yes. It's made from swifts' nests, mostly their saliva.'

'I know! Their spittle!' she exclaimed, pulling a face.

'Yes. Full of protein. Very nourishing.'

'I tried it because it's a famous delicacy.'

'What did it taste like?'

'Expensive,' she replied, and bit into a ginger biscuit.

'Some birds fly fantastic distances when they migrate,' he went on. 'The most incredible of all are the Arctic terns. They fly down to the South Pole and back every year – that's a twenty-five thousand mile round trip! And birds have the best eyesight of all animals. A hawk can see ten times more clearly than we can. Its eyes are heavier than its brain! Have you got a book about birds? This one's excellent.'

Sandy rose from his chair rather unsteadily and fetched a book from his bedside table.

'Would you like to have it?' he said, offering it to her.

Stella shrugged. 'My library is stacked up to the ceiling with hundreds of books on every subject under the sun.'

'Oh. I see.' Sandy sounded crestfallen. 'I just thought this one might interest you after what we saw today.'

'Let's have a look.' She took the book from him and leafed through the pages.

Sandy returned to his chair, gasping for breath.

'How much do you want for it?' Stella was admiring the wonderful pictures, always on the lookout for a bargain.

'Nothing,' Sandy said, rather surprised. 'It was nice of you to come all the way from London to visit me. You can have it as a gift.'

'You mean a freebie?' She was incredulous. In Stella's world everything had a price, usually quite a high one.

'Of course. I don't expect any money for it. Honestly. Go on, take it home with you.'

'All right,' she said, without adding "thank you", and put it in her briefcase.

Sandy smiled with pleasure.

'Will you be able to come and visit me again?'

'My days are very busy,' she replied evasively.

She mistrusted all friendly gestures. What was behind them?

'I'll see what I can do.'

When the time came for Stella to leave, Sandy and his mother came outside to wave her goodbye.

'OK, Bollards, let's go home,' Stella said, getting into her car.

'Right-oh, Miss.'

But the next moment she froze on hearing a familiar voice.

'*I can't cope. I just can't cope.*'

Stella sat forward and peered out of the window.

'That was my Aunt Zany! Has she turned up?'

Sandy laughed. 'No. It was only Batty.'

The parrot was perched on Sandy's shoulder.

'But that's impossible. It sounded exactly like my Aunt Zany.'

'*I can't cope. I just can't cope,*' Batty repeated, imitating Aunt Zany's voice with uncanny precision.

'That's what *she* says! How did Batty learn that?'

'Oh he knows hundreds of phrases. He keeps coming out with new ones all the time.'

'*Silly idiot! Stupid fool!*' Batty added for good measure.

'Bye-bye, Stella. It was nice to meet you,' Mrs Bottom called out, waving to her.

'Cheerio! Come and visit me again soon!' Sandy yelled. And then his mother turned his wheelchair around and took him back inside the house.

As Stella's car purred away from Happy Days, she sat bolt upright in her seat, astonished at hearing Aunt Zany's voice coming out of an African Grey parrot.

At first, Stella felt angry. Her visit was what she termed a washout. The yellow cello had stayed in the boot.

Normally, that single fact would have made her grimly determined never to visit Sandy again.

However, only seconds later she was giggling as she recalled the cake crumb shooting out of her mouth and landing – plonk – in Sandy's cup of tea, and his helpless laughter.

And there was the warm sunlight on the trees, the woody smells, Dottie the donkey eating grass, the green yaffingale, and Sandy's infectious enthusiasm for every kind of bird.

And what about the beautiful book he had given her?

She took it from her briefcase, opened it and was at once totally engrossed.

Before she knew it, her car was passing through the gates of her drive.

As it pulled up outside her magnificent home, she noticed Mr Beeswax leaving. He gave her a cautious wave.

She was in such a good mood, she waved back.

Running up the steps, she bumped into her aunt at the front door.

'Ooh, sorry, Aunt Zany. Hasn't it been a beautiful day!'

'You're smiling, Stella,' she observed anxiously. 'Are you feeling all right?'

'Of course I am. What was that solicitor doing here?'

Her aunt blushed as red as a carnation.

'He came to see me.'

'Why?'

'To invite me to go to a film with him, "forthwith". I said no.'

'Well, I hope he doesn't charge me for the visit.'

'How was your trip?' her aunt asked, anxious for the cello.

'Really good. I was given this book. Look. It's terrific.'

Stella showed her Sandy's book and described the fun she'd had with him, bird-watching, feeding a donkey, and what it felt like to have a parrot walk up her arm and sit on her shoulder. No mention of the yellow cello.

'I might go again next week,' she announced with a smile.

Hearing her own words, Stella was as taken aback as her aunt was.

'That's odd,' she thought. 'I hate the company of children, but I had a jolly time with Sandy. He's fun.'

However, her smile faded as she thought of his mysterious illness, the run-down, ramshackle cottage and how worried and tired Mrs Bottom had looked, and she felt very sad.

'Is this what they called "mixed feelings"?' she wondered.

And then there was the baffling business of her aunt's voice coming out of a parrot.

'Aunt Zany, did you ring Mrs Bottom last week about swapping my cello for Sandy's parrot?'

'I did indeed. She said no and hung up on me.'

'Did you speak to Batty as well?'

'Did I speak to whom?'

'To Batty. Sandy's talking parrot.'

'Did I have a telephone conversation with his parrot?'

'He must have heard your voice because he did a really good imitation of you. What did you say?'

Aunt Zany was so confused, she had to sit down.

'Forgive me but I don't quite understand. Are you asking me, seriously, if I had a telephone conversation with a parrot?'

'Yes, his name's Batty. What did you say to him? Try to remember.'

'Stella, I am sure all kinds of weird and wonderful things are possible these days, but talking to a parrot over the phone about a cello is not one of them.'

'Never mind. It doesn't matter.'

Stella went to bed that night feeling so puzzled that it's no wonder she had a strange dream.

Dottie the donkey was wandering about her garden eating all the flowers.

'Leave my plants alone!' Stella protested.

Dottie ignored her.

'It's pointless speaking to animals, anyhow, because they can't talk back. That's why they're called dumb animals.'

Dottie looked her smack in the eye, and said, 'I certainly don't speak to people like you.'

'Why not?' asked Stella, indignantly.

'Because you think I'm stupid. Do you talk to people who think *you're* stupid?'

'I didn't say you were stupid,' Stella answered, trying to remember very quickly if she had.

'You called your maid a stupid donkey last week. I heard you.'

'I didn't mean it personally. It was – just a remark.'

'It was an insult to all donkeys. Don't say it again, please.'

'All right, I won't – if you stop eating my flowers.'

'Did you have a question for me?' Dottie asked, helping herself to another marigold.

'Yes. How much is my cello worth exactly?'

'It's worth a great deal of time and study. It's worth all the effort you are prepared to put into it. But you have to pay.'

'Pay how much?'

'Pay attention!'

'But it's of no value.'

'Learn to play it and you will get *enormous* value out of it,' Dottie insisted. '*Tremendous* value! *Fantastic* value!'

And with that she brayed, kicked both hind legs in the air and frisked away into the night.

Stella woke up, opened one eye and looked at her cello.

'Donkeys can't speak,' she mumbled drowsily. 'Not real

donkeys. But Dottie spoke to me, even if it was just a dream. Should I take it seriously?'

There was only one way to find out.

The next day she flew to New York to see the best – and, of course, the most expensive – psychiatrist in the world, Dr U R Nutts.

'What did my dream *mean*?' she asked him.

'You were not talking to a donkey, Stella. You were talking to yourself.'

'Excuse me, Dr Nutts, I was talking to a donkey. Not an actual one, it's true. A dream donkey. But I spoke to it. And it talked back. It was as real and believable as you are! Please explain what the dream *meant*.'

She was already impatient with him. She didn't trust him because he had a shiny, bald head and bushy eyebrows.

'Let me tell you something about dreams, Stella. They don't happen to us. We *make* them happen. We invent all the people, objects and places in our dreams, however strange or puzzling.'

'Go on.'

'What I'm saying is, you created that donkey inside your head, while you were asleep. In other words, *you* were the donkey. The next question is – *Why* were you being a donkey? What were you *saying* to yourself?'

'Just a moment,' she said.

A dangerous look had come into Stella's eyes.

'Donkeys are considered to be stupid.'

'That's the general opinion,' agreed Dr Nutts, calmly.

'And stubborn.'

'Correct,' nodded Dr Nutts, wisely.

'And tiresomely foolish.'

'Indeed,' affirmed Dr Nutts, ruefully.

'And you say *I* was the donkey?'

'Precisely,' smiled Dr Nutts, pleasantly.

Stella grabbed her briefcase and stood up.

'You're fired!' she shouted, and marched out of his office and flew back to London.

CHAPTER NINE

A Dream Cello

At the airport, Mr Steele greeted Stella with a dazzling smile and terrible news.

'A lady rang you, called Mrs Button or something. She said her son was taken seriously ill and had to go into hospital.'

'You mean Mrs Bottom?'

'Could have been.'

'I must give her a call.'

'You can't. She said her phone's been cut off because she can't afford to pay her bill. She was ringing from the hospital.'

'I must visit Sandy. Which hospital?'

'Erm... I think it began with a P.'

'Didn't you write it down?'

'I couldn't find a biro. Then she ran out of change and the line went dead. She'll probably ring back later. What was New York like? Did you buy lots of stuff?'

Mrs Bottom didn't ring back later, so Stella ordered Bollards to whisk her off to *Happy Days* to find out what was wrong.

There was no response when she knocked on the front door – all was dark and silent.

She managed to track Sandy down at the nearby hospital, Iver Cross General, but by the time she arrived it was early evening.

The pretty, young nurse who was on night duty, Pinkie Lastick, refused to let Stella see him.

'Sorry. He's resting and can't be disturbed.'

Stella was feeling tired and bad-tempered – her old self.

'Now listen properly. My name is Stella Wishbone and I'm very rich. Sandy is my friend and I want to see him at once. Where is his room?'

'I'm sorry, Miss Fishbone. No visitors allowed. Ring tomorrow.'

'My name is not Fishbone, it's Wishbone! Where is Sandy's mother? I'll pay her phone bills. And I'll pay to have Sandy cured. I'm the richest girl in the world. Don't you understand?!'

'Please keep your voice down. Mrs Bottom is having a well-earned sleep. Try to understand. There are some things in life that money can't buy. We are doing everything possible for Sandy. Now go home like a good little girl.'

'Don't call me a little girl!' Stella screamed, stamping her foot. 'When I want something I get it and I want to see Sandy, so don't tell me to go home!'

Stella in a rage was an alarming sight, like a boiling kettle filling a kitchen with steam and blowing a whistle that can be heard two houses away.

Nurse Lastick had to call for help. It took two male orderlies to drag Stella out of the reception area, by which time she had woken up all the patients on the ground floor and knocked over a cleaner's bucket full of soapy water.

She was in such a dreadful mood when she got home, it's no wonder she had another disturbing dream that night.

It began like the previous night's dream, but this time she was talking to Dottie the donkey in the field.

'I *told* you what to do with the yellow cello!' Dottie said, stamping her right hoof. 'Can't you understand plain English? You must learn to play it. You haven't even touched it yet.'

'I have,' objected Stella.

'No, you haven't. Not once. Learn to play the cello! There's no time to lose!'

'*No time to lose!*' repeated Batty the parrot, who was flying above their heads.

Dottie was looking at the far horizon, her eyes wide with fear. She brayed in loud alarm, then turned and raced away in the opposite direction.

Stella wondered what had frightened the donkey. She peered into the distance at the dark blue hills.

At first she couldn't make anything out.

Then she saw it.

The entire hillside was moving. In fact, it was a great wall of water, like a tidal wave, and it was rushing towards her, crushing and consuming everything in its path – fields, trees and houses.

She froze with fear. She wanted to run but her legs were like logs, rooted to the earth. She could only watch the terrifying mass of water coming nearer and nearer.

'Excuse me,' said a deep voice. 'Penny for your thoughts.'

Stella turned around. Nobody was there.

However, leaning casually against the fence and smiling at her, was her yellow cello.

Stella screamed, 'Stop grinning at me like that, you great, useless instrument!'

The cello gave a low chuckle.

'I may be a great instrument but I'm far from useless, as you will find out.'

It then stood up and flew smoothly to her side.

'Don't be afraid. Hop on, and we'll simply rise above the whole thing!'

'I don't take orders from pieces of wood,' Stella replied haughtily. But was this a time to be choosy?

'Some of my best friends are made of wood,' the cello said. 'Hazel Nutt. Very polished. Laurel Grove. Always branching out.'

Stella was suspicious. 'A talking parrot, a talking donkey and now a talking cello! This has to be a dream.'

'Hop on,' the cello urged. 'Presto!'

'*Hop on, silly idiot!*' cried Batty, wheeling round and round Stella's head. Or was it Aunt Zany? It was beginning to look like her.

'*I can't cope!*' it screeched, and then zoomed off in the same direction Dottie had vanished.

Stella sat herself astride the middle of the cello.

'Hold very tight, please,' it said, and immediately rose into the air and flew over the field.

To save herself from falling off, Stella clung to its neck with both hands as they soared above the hedges and skimmed across the roof of the pub.

'People talk about getting carried away by music. Is this what they mean?' Stella wondered.

'Exactly. You are being transported with delight,' the cello answered, reading her thoughts exactly. 'It's most uplifting. Shall I sing you a soaring melody?'

As they rose higher over the trees, the cello began to hum a beautiful waltz tune.

'Watch out for the church steeple!' Stella cried, as the cello flew within inches of the weathervane atop the ancient spire.

The brass cockerel was swinging around crazily, pointing North, West, East and South, as if it had lost all sense of direction.

'*Cock-a-doodle-doo!*' it crowed. '*I just don't know which way to turn next!*'

Stella kicked it angrily as she flew past and set it spinning like a humming-top.

Heavy storm clouds crowded the sky and the wind howled strangely.

Two large seagulls glided inquisitively alongside for a while. One of them looked at Stella through a pair of binoculars.

'What an interesting bird,' it remarked, and then flew off with its companion.

Stella glanced down at the earth far below, which now appeared more like a coloured map with its network of roads and fields.

'My friend Sandy lives in that cottage down there! The water's rushing towards it. He'll be drowned! We must save him!'

The cello banked hard to the left and then plunged into a steep dive, humming a speedy *To The Rescue* theme.

Down, down, down it flew and in through the open front window of Happy Days.

And there was Sandy, sitting in his wheelchair reading a book.

'Sandy!' Stella shouted, 'Where's your mother?!'

The whole house was shaking with the force of the approaching water.

'She ran away,' he replied, removing his spectacles wistfully.

'Climb on behind me! Quick!' she gasped.

Sandy seemed oddly unconcerned about the impending danger. He smiled, stood up slowly and sat on the cello behind

Stella, holding onto her waist as if he were riding pillion on a motorbike. They immediately flew out through the window and up into the thundery sky.

Only two seconds later, Stella glanced down and saw the immense body of water overwhelm the little cottage, which disappeared beneath the all-devouring flood.

'Flying is wonderful!' Sandy laughed, as they soared almost vertically upwards. 'Aren't I lucky to have friends in high places?' he joked.

A flock of peculiar-looking birds suddenly appeared from nowhere, all travelling in the same direction.

'Those aren't birds,' Stella exclaimed after a closer look. 'They're books!'

'Yes. That one at the front is a red illustrated hard-cover,' Sandy explained, knowledgeably. 'And the others are common spotted paper-backs. They're flying south for the winter sales.'

Many thousands appeared making a tremendous din, a migrating multitude, flapping their pages and chattering to each other in a language which Stella found pleasing but puzzling.

Finally, a solitary notebook fluttered past them.

'That straggler's a little ring-binder,' Sandy pointed out.

'We aren't home and dry yet,' Stella said. 'We're heading straight for an enormous cloud. Look!'

She pointed to a threatening storm cloud directly in front of them, deep purple and grey and as huge as a mountain.

The cello's music grew louder and faster.

'Slow down, or we'll crash into it!' she yelled.

'Don't worry, Stella,' said the cello. 'It's only a cloud. Clouds are nothing. Everything is going to be all right.'

'No, it's not!' she cried. 'Look out! We're going to hit it!'

'Flying is great!' shouted Sandy cheerfully, as the cello gathered speed and flew faster and faster and faster!

'Stop!' cried Stella.

'Here we go!' yelled Sandy.

And they flew headlong into the solid-looking cloud.

Thud!

Stella woke up.

Darkness. Silence. She was safe in her bed.

'Oh, thank goodness it was just a dream,' she said out loud, but the music that the cello had been playing still echoed inside her head...

To make sure everything really was all right, as the cello had assured her, she sat up and looked around the room.

The light of the full moon shone through her balcony windows, transforming all the familiar objects of daytime into silvery, shadowy mysteries.

A grey armchair with pale blue silk cushions became an iceberg floating on a motionless sea. The oval mirror on her wardrobe door looked like the entrance to an underwater cave. And the table lamp on her desk, with its wide shade, was like a weird little tree growing on a planet a billion miles away.

And of course, leaning in the corner, but still appearing very much like itself, was the yellow cello.

However, its ability to fly through the air singing songs, even if only in a dream, had produced a powerful effect. Stella now looked at the cello in quite a different light.

She clambered out of bed and went over to the cello. What had Dottie the donkey said in her dream? –

'You haven't even touched it yet.'

'It's true,' Stella thought. 'I haven't touched it once. Aunt Zany's carried it up and down stairs. The maids have moved it while they've been cleaning. Bollards put it in the boot of the car when I visited Sandy. But I've never touched it. I wonder if something extraordinary will happen if I do!'

She reached forward until the tip of her finger was only a fraction of an inch from its surface.

The moonlight stood absolutely still. The summer air held its breath. The whole room braced itself for a terrible shock. She glanced over her shoulder, half expecting to see someone standing there.

But no, she was alone. Was it just her imagination, or was there an atmosphere all around her of intense interest in this particular moment? It was unspoken, unseen – but she was sure something was there.

Can you hear silence? Can you see the invisible? Her sleepy

head swam with confusing, new thoughts. And then the donkey's words echoed clearly in her mind –

'Learn to play the cello and you'll get enormous value out of it.'

And Stella touched the yellow cello.

CHAPTER TEN

First the Good News

Stella was eating her breakfast in bed the following morning –
fruit-juice, porridge, marmalade on toast and a banana, neatly
laid out on a white linen cloth on a silver tray.

There was a rattling noise and Aunt Zany popped in to see if
everything was all right.

'I *was* going to fly to Italy this weekend to buy some shoes.'

'But Stella, you've got hundreds of pairs!'

'They're all boring. Anyway, I've ditched that idea. Instead,
I've decided to learn to play the cello.'

Aunt Zany clutched her bosom with delight. It rattled.

'Oh Stella, that's wonderful news! But I think it takes longer
than a weekend, from what I've heard.'

'I mean I'm going to *start* to learn this weekend.'

Stella's head was still full of her peculiar dream.

'Can cellos fly about?'

Her Aunt was startled by this question. 'I don't understand.
Fly about where?'

'Never mind. I've made an appointment to see the top cello
teacher in London, Wanda Backenforth.'

'I can't tell you how happy I am to hear this,' said Aunt Zany,
her eyes filling with tears of joy. 'But what caused you to change
your mind?'

'Oh, just something someone said.'

'Who?'

She wasn't going to admit that it was a donkey, so she skilfully
changed the subject.

'Where is Stir?'

Aunt Zany pursed her lips, as if she had just swallowed a
particularly bitter pill.

'Mr Steele hasn't arrived yet. In fact, he's never on time. I've made a few enquiries about him, Stella, and I regret to say there's something not quite right about him.'

'What do you mean?'

There was a knock at the door.

'I'll tell you later.'

It was Stir. He was really, *really* excited about the plan he had worked out to make Stella even more rich.

'Have you ever heard of the Cripes Diamond?'

'No,' said Stella.

'It's the biggest diamond in the whole world. Almost as big as a rugby football! It doubles its value two hundred percent every year, and it's up for sale. If you bought it, you could sell it next year and make a really huge profit.'

'What a brilliant idea! Let's do it,' said Stella, swept away by Stir's enthusiasm. 'Ring me on my mobile. We can discus the details while I'm being driven to my cello lesson.'

'Just one moment,' interrupted Aunt Zany. 'Mr Steele, how much money would Stella have to pay for this Cripes Diamond?'

'Oh, about seventy or eighty,' he said vaguely.

'Seventy or eighty what?'

'Million.'

'Seventy or eighty million *pounds?!*' she gasped. 'But that would mean having to sell everything she owns! Even this house! It's out of the question.'

Stir's smile didn't fade, exactly. It sort of froze into a solid clamp, like a steel trap.

'I believe Stella's money is hers to spend as she thinks best.'

'That doesn't mean I would allow her to do something as foolish and ill-advised as this.'

'I think we'll have to let Stella decide that for herself, Miss Handlebar.'

'Aunt Zany, please don't interfere. Stir's idea isn't foolish. It's brilliant.'

'Stella, you aren't seriously considering – ? You're not going to *do* this?'

'Yes I am. I think it's a terrific scheme, and just what I need to cheer me up – more money.'

'But it's sheer madness,' Aunt Zany protested weakly, wringing her hands. 'I can't cope, I just can't cope. Excuse me. I must take several pills.'

As she rattled out of the room, Stir continued to watch her with a fixed smile. He was remembering a question he had recently asked Stella about Aunt Zany –

'What would happen to her if she suddenly stopped taking the pills?'

'I should think she'd probably explode.'

His blue eyes continued to glitter with their shatter-proof, non-stick charm.

'What an unusual cello,' said Wanda Backenforth. 'It's yellow.'

Stella wanted to shout, 'I know it is! You're fired!'

To stop herself, she pressed her fingers against her lips.

'Do you have a bad tooth?' asked Miss Backenforth.

Stella shook her head.

'Then please sit properly with your hands in your lap, Stella, there's a good little girl.'

Stella almost blurted out, 'Don't call me a little girl!' She clutched her mouth with both hands this time.

'Are you going to be sick?' asked the concerned Miss Backenforth.

Again, Stella shook her head.

They were sitting facing each other in the cluttered music room of Miss Backenforth's Victorian house. On the walls were a number of framed and signed photographs of former pupils who had become famous cello players.

'As I was saying,' continued Miss Backenforth, 'this is a most interesting cello; lots of character. I wonder what wood it's made of. It has a sheen like the inside of buttercups.'

She played a series of deep notes that made every bone in Stella's body tickle with vibrations.

'A gorgeous tone, as well,' she added.

Miss Backenforth was a fierce-looking lady with mousy hair, buck teeth, piggy eyes, and a single mole on her double chin. By Stella's exacting standards, she was not pretty.

Nor, in her opinion, did she dress well. Her clothes looked ill-matched. She was wearing a lime-green jacket over a strawberry-pink blouse, and an aubergine-purple skirt with cherry-red spots.

'She looks like a bag of mixed fruit and veg,' Stella thought to herself.

But my goodness, something beautiful happened when she played the cello. It didn't just produce notes, it produced a voice. And the voice sang.

She obviously loved the instrument, and she had the wonderful knack of kindling the same feeling in her pupils.

But Stella didn't like the look of her.

'So far,' she thought, 'I am not impressed.'

'Where do we start?' Stella asked, in her let's-get-down-to-business voice.

Miss Backenforth stared sternly at the incredibly self-assured child in front of her, slightly taken aback by her air of authority.

'I'm afraid this cello will be a little too large for you to start learning on.'

'I learn on this one, or I don't learn at all,' Stella stated flatly.

'As you wish. You seem to know your own mind, Stella.'

'So what do I do, Miss Backenforth?'

'You sit as I was sitting, with the cello like this, between your knees, holding the neck – so – and with the bow in your other hand – so.'

Stella grappled with the instrument resolutely. When she made up her mind to tackle a challenge, nothing short of an earthquake or a force ten hurricane could stop her.

'Shall I do what you just did?'

'Try. It's not quite as easy as it looks, but once you get used to the – '

'I was watching. You did this.'

She drew the bow slowly across the thickest string, producing a wonderfully resonant A natural.

'Excellent, Stella,' said Miss Backenforth with a smile. 'Again.'

'Oh, by the way, I have a question. Can cellos fly?'

Miss Backenforth's smile was replaced by a look of blank astonishment.

'Did you say fly?'

'Yes.'

'The answer is no. What in blue blazes gave you that idea?'

'Just thought I'd ask,' Stella said.

'Another note please. You're doing splendidly, my dear.'

'Wait a minute. You put your finger on the string at the top – here. And you wiggled it up and down at the same time. Like this.'

And she produced a B natural, this time with a warm 'vibrato' – a slight wobble in the sound, instead of an even, pure note, like the difference between straight hair and wavy hair.

'Have you played the cello before?' asked Miss Backenforth.

'No,' said Stella.

'But that note you produced was wonderfully rich!'

'Rich!' Stella's eyes lit up like fireworks. 'I think I'm going to enjoy this.'

Stella's progress over the next two months was good. She practised every day and was soon able to play simple tunes.

During each lesson, Wanda Backenforth would wander back and forth and make encouraging comments.

'You have a natural gift for the cello. It's in your blood. Is anyone in your family musical?'

'I'd rather not discuss my family. They are all weird.'

And every night the yellow cello would fly in and out of Stella's dreams, playing wonderful melodies all by itself.

Stella also began to notice something odd.

Often when she returned home from a lesson, she would spot Mr Beeswax leaving. The 'stupid solicitor' would give her a friendly wave as her car swept past him. But every time she asked why he had called, her aunt would stammer incoherently and stuff more pills into her mouth.

Finally the truth came out.

'What is going on?' demanded Stella.

'Mr Beeswax,' her aunt admitted, 'has asked me to marry him. Forthwith.'

'Why?' exclaimed Stella.

'Heaven knows.' And she blushed like a guilty pie thief.

'Does he think you're rich?' Stella asked in amazement, which was extremely rude but completely in character.

'No. He says he is hopelessly in love with me.'

There was a slight hint of boasting in her voice.

'Are you in love with him?'

Her aunt's face now went the colour of peeled beetroot.

'What a silly question! How can you ask?'

'So what did you say?'

'I said no. I said I wouldn't even contemplate such an idea because I have to look after you. So that's the end of the subject. He'll not be visiting us again. Now off you go to the library. Your factory manager is waiting to see you. But wash your hands first.'

A month later, Stella was returning home in her chauffeur driven limo after another cello lesson.

As she chatted to Stirling Steele on her mobile phone, she ploughed her way through the Business Section in the Telegraph.

'According to Miss Backenforth, I have a real feeling for the cello.'

'Do you like her?'

'Well, I suppose so. She's ugly, and she wears awful clothes. But she is a good teacher,' she said, idly turning the pages.

'Ugly people make me uncomfortable,' Mr Steele answered. 'I'm not a snob, honestly, but I feel more at ease with attractive, nice-looking people. Like yourself, if I may be allowed to say.'

Unseen by him, Stella beamed with pleasure.

'Ugly people can't *help* being ugly,' she said, with unusual generosity. 'I just wish they weren't. They probably do as well.' And then she frowned.

'I wonder how Sandy is.'

'Who?' asked Mr Steele.

'The boy with the parrot. I was so angry the hospital nurse wouldn't let me see him, I didn't bother to go again. Shall I send his mother some money?'

Mr Steele was amazed. 'What for?'

'To pay her phone bill. They're very poor.'

'Mmm. I'd be careful if I were you. She might start asking for more and more.'

'Oh yes. I hadn't thought of that. Thanks for the warning.'
Stella picked up the Financial Times.

'That's the trouble with poor people,' Mr Steele continued.
'They're always grumbling about the high price of everything.
It's really boring. Rich people are far more fun to be with because
they have a marvellous sense of humour. Have you noticed? When
a rich person makes a joke, everybody laughs. It's true.'

There was no reply.

'Hallo? Stella? Are you still there?'

The silence continued. Stella's eye had been caught by a
headline.

Stella Wishbone – Poor Little Rich Girl
Shocking new secret revealed
Turn to page 7

She turned savagely to page seven and read the article with
mounting disbelief and anger, just as her car stopped outside her
house.

She sprang out, ran up the steps and burst through the front
door.

'Aunt Zany! Aunt Zany! Come here immediately!'

She tore off her coat and flung it at her new maid, Anita
Clozzit.

'Where is my aunt?' she yelled.

'In the kitchen,' the maid answered, almost paralysed with
terror. 'She's not well.'

Stella marched furiously into the kitchen and there was Aunt
Zany.

The door of her pill cupboard was wide open and the shelves
completely bare. Her aunt was clinging to the bottom shelf with
one hand, as if dangling from the edge of a cliff.

'My pills! My pills! They've all gone!' she wailed. 'I can't
cope, I just can't cope!'

She sank to the floor, moaning and clutching her head with
her mitten-covered fingers.

'Aunt Zany, get up this instant! I need to talk to you about
something extremely serious.'

Aunt Zany gazed up at Stella with a tragic expression, like a
dying duck in a thunderstorm.

'They've gone. Disappeared. All my pills. Someone has taken them. I shall die, slowly and suddenly. I know it!'

Just at that moment they were joined by Mr Steele.

'It's him!' Aunt Zany wailed, pointing a shaking finger.

'He's stolen my pills! He wants to kill me!'

'What on earth are you talking about, Miss Handlebar?' he asked in a smooth voice, smiling innocently. 'Aren't you feeling well?'

Aunt Zany clasped Stella's hand piteously.

'I beg you. I must have my pills or I shall die. I can't do anything without them. I can't hum rice puddings, or cook pop songs, or anything! I shall become unhinged!'

'Aunt Zany, your mind is wandering. Get a grip.'

'It's my pills – I can't even *think* without them. I can't lick bubbles or blow stamps or anything.'

'You're delirious. You mean blow bubbles or lick stamps. Stir, drive over to Dr Ponytail for her pill prescription, and buy them at the chemist's.'

'Sure. No problem. I'm on my way.'

He turned to face the mirror, took out a comb and ran it through his hair, which was already perfect.

'As soon as possible,' begged Aunt Zany.

'OK. It'll take me about three quarters of an hour in this traffic. Try to hold on, Miss Handlebar.'

He then adjusted his tie carefully.

'Hurry,' groaned Aunt Zany. 'I'm sinking fast.'

'I'll be back,' he added, removing a piece of fluff from his shoulder, 'in just a jiff.'

And he strolled out of the kitchen. Slowly.

'Aunt Zany, those pills make you very forgetful. You must have thrown them away yourself without knowing what you were doing.'

'Why would I throw them away?' she gasped. 'No. It was him. He wants me out of this house. He wants me *dead!*'

'Why would Stir want you dead?'

'Because I'm on to him. He's not who he says he is. He's a liar and a confidence trickster.'

Stella's face was white with anger.

'This is nonsense, Aunt Zany. Stir is a nice, honest and really sincere person. And I *like* him.'

'No, I was going to tell you. I checked up on his background, his school, his former employers, his home address. And I found – *nothing!* Not one, single thing about him is real. Not even his name. He's a complete fraud!'

'For goodness' sake, I've had enough of this,' protested Stella. 'You've gone too far. We'll continue this conversation when you've had a cup of tea and calmed down. Where's that stupid donkey of a maid? I mean – that clever, intelligent maid who doesn't in the least bit resemble a donkey.'

Ten minutes later, Aunt Zany was lying on the sofa in the drawing-room, sipping a strong cup of tea.

Stella was standing by the fireplace, glowering at her.

'Is this true?'

'Is what true, Stella?'

'What it says about me here,' she answered.

She marched over to her aunt, plonked the newspaper on her lap and pointed to it.

'On page seven.'

Aunt Zany glanced fearfully at the article and recoiled.

'Well?' Stella insisted.

Aunt Zany quivered with fear like a plucked harp string.

'You mustn't believe what's printed in the newspapers. Most of the stories are practical jokes to entertain the readers.'

But Stella's gaze was aimed straight at her like a long, frozen carrot.

'Is it true?' she repeated, threateningly.

'Yes, it's true.'

'My mother did *not* die after I was born?'

'No.'

'You told me she did.'

'I need my pills.'

'You lied to me. Everyone lied to me!'

'I must have my pills.'

'Where did my mother go? Tell me what happened to her.'

'She ran away. She spent her last seven years on this earth

living alone in a remote lighthouse, her only companions a grey parrot – and a yellow cello.'

Stella gasped. 'You mean… '

'Yes. Olive Underfelt – was your mother!'

CHAPTER ELEVEN

The Awful, Terrible Truth

'I was going to tell you the awful, terrible truth one day. When you were older.'

'Tell me *now!*'

'Very well.'

Aunt Zany's large, sad eyes filled with tears, as she searched her pill-fogged memory.

'It all began so wonderfully, like a fairy story. Imagine, two little sisters, born and raised in a magnificent, tropical forest in east Africa. One was Mad and the other Zany – named after islands off the coast of Africa – Madagascar and Zanzibar.

'Our dear father and mother were English doctors who ran a health centre in Tanzania. Dad's name was Rusty Handlebar and Mum's name was Pearl.

'They were wonderful, dedicated souls, as poor as church mice but contented.

'As dad used to say, *"All you need in life is a smile on your face, a song in your heart, and a banana in your hand."* He was a cheerful, uncomplicated soul.'

'Africa!' Stella exclaimed, remembering Sandy Bottom's account of the two sisters.

'It was you and my mother who found the parrot's egg.'

'Yes. It fell from an abandoned nest in a hollow podo tree. We had no idea what sort of bird might be inside, but we took it home and hatched it – and out came Batty!'

'Why did you call him Batty?'

'We didn't. We called him Bahati – which is the Swahili word for 'lucky'. And he certainly was! If we hadn't found the egg and kept it warm, he would never have hatched out. However, Bahati soon got shortened to Batty, and so the three of us were Mad, Zany and Batty! People nicknamed us the Crazy Club.'

'What was my mother like?' Stella asked, in a low, serious voice.

'Oh Stella, she was delightful. Although we were sisters, we were totally different. Mad was very pretty, full of fun, always making people laugh. And so bright and musical. Whereas I was the plain one. Clumsy, shy and tone deaf. But we were devoted to each other, and as happy as the sun was hot – which was very! – me looking after Batty, and Maddy playing her lovely yellow cello.'

'Just a moment,' Stella interrupted. 'She was playing a yellow cello? In the middle of a tropical forest?'

'Yes,' said Aunt Zany, with a girlish giggle. 'Bizarre, isn't it?' Stella was not amused.

'Where did this yellow cello come from? Don't tell me it fell out of a tree as well.'

'This is what happened. As a child, our mother had learnt to play that instrument. But, sadly, when she came to Africa, her cello was eaten by termites.

'"If only we could afford to buy another cello," she said, 'I would teach you girls how to play. It's such a beautiful sound."

'The idea never appealed to me, but Maddy was dead keen to learn. She was always humming tunes.

'Now it so happened that there was a wonderful old carpenter living nearby, whose name was Albie Senior. He started to go blind, so our parents operated on him in order to save his dear sight.

'Maddy used to visit Mr Senior while his eyes were still bandaged. She made up funny little nonsense songs and sang them to Albie to cheer him up.'

'I would find that very irritating,' Stella remarked.

'Oh far from it! He said he loved her jolly, jaunty jingles. They delighted him no end.

'"When I'm better, little Maddy," he said, "I shall carve a present for you. Tell me what you would like."

'Guess what Mad asked for.'

'A cello, by any chance?'

'Yes! *More than anything in the world,"* she said, *"I would love to have a cello."*

'Now, it so happened that Albie hadn't the faintest idea what a cello *was*, let alone what one looked or sounded like. Do you know what he did? When his sight was restored, he found a photograph of a cello in a magazine and copied it exactly! Enormously clever, when you think about it. That's why it's a bit unusual, as people say.

'And when he gave it to Mad, he said, *"I have glued magic into its joints so that it will bring good fortune and happiness to whoever plays it."*

'I've since wondered if he glued the magic in upside-down because of what happened to Mad later...

'However, for the time being, we *were* happy. Blissfully happy. Joyously happy! I decided to be a vet when I grew up, so Dad taught me about animals. And Mum gave Mad cello lessons because she hoped to become a professional cellist one day. Ours was an enchanted, carefree world of deep forests, wild animals, music and sunshine... '

Aunt Zany's face was lit with an expression of innocent delight. For a fleeting moment, she looked twenty years younger. But her smile soon faded and a look of profound sorrow came over her.

'Until one terrible day.' She could hardly continue. 'A dreadful accident took place. Both of our beloved parents were drowned when a huge wave overturned their boat on Lake Tanganyika.'

'How strange,' Stella thought, remembering the menacing flood in her dream.

'People told us we would have to be sent home to England. Home? Our home was Africa, and the echoing forest. I still think about it all these years later.'

'Go on,' Stella said, grimly.

'London was a rude awakening – cold and gloomy. And so were the people. We were sent to live with the Savages in Putney.'

'The who?' asked Stella.

'Sam and Pam Savage – two distant relatives. Mad used

to call them Spam and Jam Sandwich – not to their faces, of course! They took us in as if it were an unpleasant duty, which it probably was. We arrived on their doorstep carrying our pitiful few belongings: a grey parrot, a yellow cello, and one pink sponge bag each.'

'Is that all?' Stella asked in disbelief.

'Our parents had been as penniless as the people they worked among. It didn't seem to matter then. But in London – oh dear! Batty was sent into quarantine for six months, and Mad and I were sent to a school for six years.'

She closed her eyes and shuddered.

'Sheer misery. The other children teased us for our strange ways. To them, we were more like ring-tailed lemurs than little girls. As for studying to be a vet or a cellist! – Huh! Those fond dreams were shattered. No college for us. When we left school we had to take the first jobs available. I said I enjoyed travelling and meeting people. So they put a ticket-machine round my neck and stuck me on a number 27 double-decker bus.'

'You were a bus conductor!'

'Oh, those stairs,' she groaned. 'And those fares! Stairs and fares. Day after day. Week in, week out. I nearly went potty. My one consolation was Batty. He sat on my shoulder as I shouted, *"Move along inside, please!"'*

'He travelled on the bus with you?'

'He loved it. So did the passengers. They fed him peanuts as I gave them their tickets. But I told them all how unhappy I was. *"I can't cope,"* I said. *"I just can't cope!"'*

'That's where Batty picked up that phrase!'

'Yes! And *"Fares, please! Hold very tight!"'*

'What about my mother?'

'No more cello lessons for her.'

'Why?'

'Too expensive. She got a job typing letters in a dreadful office above a factory. That's how she met your father.'

'How?'

'He owned the factory. Games, Jokes and Novelties. Then one fateful day, she knocked on his door.'

'Why?'

'To ask for a raise. He said, *"Will you marry me?"* It was madness.'

'Why?'

'Because he didn't love her. He just wanted a wife.'

'Why?'

'To work in his office for nothing. So she said, *"I will."*'

'Why?'

'To get out of that office!'

'How ironic,' Stella observed.

'He was rich but she didn't love him.'

'Why?'

'Because he was mean. But he was her only hope.'

'Why?'

'Because we couldn't pay our bills.'

Aunt Zany sighed and shook her head.

'Oh Stella, if you should ever marry a rich man – which is quite likely, in your case – marry a generous one. The mean ones aren't fun to be with. Your father was what is vulgarly termed a 'tightwad'. I'm sorry. I shouldn't speak ill of the dead.'

'Go on,' ordered Stella impatiently.

'His wedding present to Mad was an un-returned library book called *Brush Up Your Secretarial Skills*. And he was just the same when you were born. You arrived on a Friday evening. He said to Maddy, *"You can have the weekend off, but Monday morning you've got to be back in the office."*

'I could tell their marriage was doomed.

'And then, only a few years later, fate struck its final, deadly blow.

'It was a hot afternoon. Your father was away testing bungee jumping ropes. Maddy rang a plumber from Slough and asked him to unblock the S bend under her kitchen sink.

'When he arrived, they took one look at each other and – whoosh! Love at first sight.'

'A plumber!' Stella cried. 'From Slough! Was his name, by any curious chance, Mr Bottom?'

'Yes, Rocky Bottom.'

'Sandy Bottom's father!' Stella gasped. 'And the lady he ran off with was – !'

'Yes. Your mother. She lost her senses. I begged her not to go. I said, *"I hate to be a wet blanket but you'll be plunged headlong into a whirlpool of airlocks, ball valves and stopcocks. It's plumb crazy,"* I told her. *"He's just a drip."*

'Then I felt a tap on my shoulder.

' *"Put a plug in it,"* Mr Bottom said. *"Stop spouting advice. I'm going to shower Mad with love."*

'I tried to make your mother see reason. *"What will you live on?"* I asked her. *"Copper pipes and kisses? You're flushing your whole life down the drain."*

'But it was a waste of breath; she was overflowing with infatuation. So I washed my hands of the whole business. Off she went with him – a plumber's mate!'

'Where did they go?'

'To Bath.'

'I see,' said Stella sternly.

'I felt so sorry for Mrs Bottom. She had a little boy who was only a few days older than you.'

'Sandy! So *that's* how she knew we were the same age!'

'Rocky left her without a penny. Sadly my warning proved all too accurate,' Aunt Zany whimpered.

'Within a month your mother wrote to me choked with remorse. She said the whole affair was a washout.'

'What about Mr Bottom?'

'He went off late one night to attend an emergency call. Later, he phoned Maddy and promised faithfully he'd be with her between eight and twelve the next morning. She waited in all day but he never turned up.'

'An unreliable plumber,' Stella observed bitterly.

'She never saw him again.'

'In that case, why didn't my mother come home?'

'She wanted to, but your father wouldn't forgive her.'

'You mean, he took it as a personal insult.'

'You could say that, yes. He refused to have anything more to do with her. He even tore up all her photographs. Every single one.'

'That's why there are no pictures of my mother here.'

'Yes, it was awful. *"From now on,"* he shouted at me, *"your sister is dead and buried! Her name will never be mentioned in my house again!"'*

Aunt Zany's eyes filled with tears.

'*"What's more,"* he said, *"you must help me to bring up Stella. Forget about bus conducting. That's going nowhere. You will live in this house and look after your niece. But first, get rid of that horrible parrot!"*

'So, for your sake, I said goodbye to darling Batty. It nearly broke my heart.' Aunt Zany shook her head sadly.

Stella was becoming impatient.

'Go on.'

'I tried to take care of you. But what did I know about bringing up children? I couldn't cope. I just couldn't cope.'

'What did my mother do then?'

'She answered an advert in a newspaper for a lighthouse keeper. Poor, sad Mad. Overcome with guilt and remorse, she chose to live out the rest of her days at the top of a remote lighthouse, alone with her secret sorrow. She even changed her name to Olive Underfelt, so that no one would guess who she was. Or the terrible thing she had done.'

'And that's where she played the cello?'

'Yes. Her one consolation – her beloved music. I asked her if she would take care of Batty for me. She agreed. It was nice to think that she wouldn't be completely alone in that lighthouse.'

'What did she live on?'

'Seaweed, gulls' eggs and rain water – a dreary, unreliable diet. And so Mad pined away, playing her cello, until she finally died of a broken leg.'

'Don't you mean a broken heart?' Stella asked.

'No. There were a hundred and twenty-two steps in that lighthouse. It was a blessed relief, really. She could never forgive herself for deserting you.

'With the wind howling round that lonely tower, and the sea smashing wildly on the rocks below, she would pour out her feelings of grief and longing in heart-rending music on the yellow cello, pausing now and then to cry out, *"Silly idiot! Stupid fool!"* – repeated by Batty, flying round her head, *"Silly idiot! Stupid fool!"'*

'Of course, his other phrase,' Stella remembered.

'She wrote a simple, pathetic will, leaving Batty to Sandy Bottom and the yellow cello to you.'

A haunted look came over Aunt Zany's face.

'Some say that on dark, stormy nights, ships passing that empty lighthouse have heard the sound of a cello playing, and the ghostly voice of a woman, like a soul in torment, crying out to the raging tempest – *"Silly idiot! Stupid fool!"'*

And Aunt Zany wept.

CHAPTER TWELVE

The Fabulous Cripes Diamond

'Grown-ups are horrible!' Stella shouted angrily.

'They tell horrible lies! I shall never believe another word a grown-up says to me as long as I live! Except for Stir – he's the only one I can trust.'

Aunt Zany groaned feebly, as her head sank back onto the sofa pillow.

'I'm dying, Stella. My pills will come too late. Before I breathe my final breath, please say you forgive your mother. She loved you. You must believe that.'

'She deserted me! I'll never forgive her! Never, never, never, *never!*' Stella screamed.

She seized the newspaper in a frenzy and ripped it into a thousand fragments. Seconds later, it was as though a blizzard had hit the room.

'What's more, Aunt Zany, you're *not* dying. While the tea was being made, I rang your doctor. He told me your pills aren't real – they're just placebos. They've no medicine in them at all. You only *think* you need them. It's all in your mind.'

'It's not true. They keep me alive.'

'All they do is make you rattle, and I've had enough! You lied to me, Aunt Zany. I don't want you to live here any more. I've made arrangements for one of my pilots to take you away tomorrow in my pink plane.'

'Take me away where?'

'Somewhere. Anywhere. You choose. Back to Africa, if you like. I don't care where, but you've got to go. I never want to see you again! You're fired!'

'But Stella – who will look after you?'

Who, indeed.

The following day, Aunt Zany packed her suitcase and left the house, never to return.

As she bade her tearful farewell at the front door, she handed a piece of paper to Stella.

'I'm going back to Africa, as you suggested. This is my forwarding address. I shall live in the remote forest where I grew up, among the people I knew as a child. But I won't fly in your pink plane. I intend to find my own way there. All I ask of you, *beg* of you, is that you write to me. Please.'

Without even looking at it, Stella tore up the address. When she was angry nothing written on paper was safe!

'I've no intention of writing to you, and I'd rather you didn't write to me. All we have to say to each other is goodbye.'

'Oh Stella.'

And off Aunt Zany went.

Having got her own way in this matter, you might have expected Stella to be pleased. But, oddly enough, she spent the rest of the day biting back tears.

She knew in her heart that she loved her Aunt Zany more than anything in the world, in spite of the rattling.

It was painful to face the truth.

She had done something she was already deeply regretting.

The next morning, her office phone rang.

It rang and rang and rang.

Someone was late for work again.

Stella took the call. 'Yes.'

'Hallo? Is that you, Stella?'

'Who is this?'

'Oh, at last I've got through to you. It's Sandy's mother, Mrs Bottom.'

Another grown-up.

'I've tried this number a dozen times and left messages with your secretary but I've had no reply. Did you receive them?'

'Yes, I did,' she lied. 'I've been busy. What do you want?'

'It's about Sandy. He's very poorly and keeps asking when you're coming to visit him. He'd be so pleased if you could see him just for a short while. He said it would be a special treat for him if you could.'

'No, I can't. I'm flying to Vienna to buy the biggest diamond in the world.'

'Oh, I see. That sounds exciting. Perhaps, when you return, you might be able to pop in to say hallo for five minutes?'

For a moment, Stella was tempted to be nice. The moment passed.

'It's not really convenient. My diary is completely full.'

She knew her reply was unkind and spoken out of anger. But this was another grown-up who had withheld the truth about her mother. Why should she be nice? All adults were horrible. All except for one.

'Sandy wanted you to know he's being moved to a hospice. Shall I give you the address?'

'Not now. My secretary will contact you when things are quieter. Goodbye.'

And off she flew to Vienna, with the only grown-up she could trust – Stirling Steele.

'I'm in a really bad mood,' she said to Mr Steele, who was seated opposite her in the pink plane.

'Make me laugh.'

'All right,' he said.

He took off his shoes and cracked his big toe joints. He wiggled his ears. He pretended his hands were glued together. But nothing amused her. Even his gorilla impression failed to raise a smile.

'What runs round the park but never moves?' he asked her, getting a bit desperate.

'The railings,' she replied, glumly.

'A man went to his doctor. *'Help me,'* he said. *'I woke up laughing this morning and I can't stop'.* The doctor said to him, *'You must have slept in a funny position.'*'

'That's a good joke,' Stella nodded solemnly. 'I like it,' and then she sighed.

She still felt angry with her mother for abandoning her when she was a baby, and with Aunt Zany for lying to her about it. And with herself, for reasons she wouldn't admit.

'Never mind,' said Mr Steele. 'When I feel cheesed off, I try to think of something jolly that I can look forward to. Well, you've got *tomorrow* to look forward to. It's your birthday.'

'How did you know?'

'You told me. If you give me a little smile,' he went on, lowering his voice to a confidential whisper, 'I shall buy you a birthday present in Vienna.'

'A present?' she repeated, perking up slightly. 'I don't expect you to buy me a present,' she said, hoping very much that he would. Something exciting, suitable and expensive.

'But I *want* to. The only difficulty is – what do you give someone who has everything?'

'Shall I write you a list?' she asked.

'A surprise is more fun. Let... me... see... '

Mr Steele thought for a moment.

'I know what you haven't got!'

'What?' cried Stella, suddenly completely perked up.

'Ah-ha! You'll have to wait till *tomorrow* to find out!'

Stella was now smiling with pleasure.

Stirling took a glossy magazine from his briefcase.

'Would you like me to read you this article?'

'Am I mentioned in it?' Stella asked warily, afraid it might hold more nasty surprises involving her private life.

'No. It's all about the Cripes Diamond – where it was found, how it got its name in the first place. Things like that.'

'That sounds interesting.'

Mr Steele read out the eye-catching headline.

'CRIPES! WOT A WHOPPER!

'And underneath in smaller letters it says,

Does the biggest diamond in the world carry a dangerous, deadly curse?

'And underneath that, it says,

The grisly, gruesome history of *THE FABULOUS CRIPES DIAMOND!'*

'Ooh,' said Stella. 'Go on.'

She settled back comfortably in her deep-cushioned chair.

'Do you want to own the Cripes Diamond? You need to get your head examined!'

Stella gasped. 'Is that what you think?!'

'No, that's what it says here.'

He gave a nervous laugh.

'Perhaps I'd better stop,' he suggested. 'You might have second thoughts about the auction.'

'No! Keep reading. It won't put me off. I want to find out why I should get my head examined.'

'Are you sure?'

'Yes! There's nothing I like more than a challenge. And this sounds like a really big one. Go on!'

Mr Steele flashed her one of his dazzling smiles. Even so, his eyes looked anxious.

'OK then. Here goes.

'This week, the planet's richest millionaires will fly to Vienna to bid for the world's biggest diamond.

'Yesterday, from his luxury London flat, famous jewel dealer Jack Potts declared:

'They must all be COMPLETELY CRAZY! Why? I'll tell you why. Because, according to reliable gossip, every previous owner of this diamond has suffered a horrible fate. I wouldn't touch it with the longest bargepole in the Guinness Book of Records!'

'One top science expert, Noah Lottafax, agreed.

'Superstition is utter rubbish, but this stone should carry a health warning. It is genuinely cursed. I feel ill just thinking about it.'

'Can this be true? First, a few facts about diamonds:

*1. Diamond is the **hardest** substance in all of nature.*
        EXPECT NO PITY!

*2. It is the **purest** substance in all of nature, and yet it attracts evil.*
        YOU HAVE BEEN WARNED!

*3. A diamond can cut glass and steel, but a hammer blow can **shatter** it.*
        HANDLE WITH CARE!

*4. If left in sunlight, diamonds **glow** in the dark.*

HIDE SAFELY!
5. *A diamond can catch **fire** at high temperature.*
DON'T BURN YOUR FINGERS!
6. *A diamond is a paradox of nature. It is made of carbon*
*– a common material but in a very **rare** form.*
DON'T BE FOOLED!'

Stella shivered with delight.

'I've gone all goose-bumps,' she chuckled. 'I consider myself thoroughly warned. Go on!'

CHAPTER THIRTEEN

Unlucky for Some

Stella wriggled deeper into her luxurious aeroplane seat.

Mr Steele cleared his throat and continued to read aloud.

'The true origin of the Cripes Diamond is uncertain. The most often repeated story tells how the gem was presented as a gift to none other than Queen Elizabeth I of England by a foreign prince who was hoping to marry her.

'Rendered almost dumbstruck by its staggering size, she is supposed to have blurted out, 'Cripes!' Hence its name.

'However, this charming fable does not bear close examination. For a start, Good Queen Bess, as she was affectionately known (even though she had dozens of people's heads chopped off!), was never lost for words. Ever. She always had a queenly quip on the tip of her tongue, or a snide aside up her puffed sleeve for every occasion.

'Also the word cripes did not exist then. It is a slang term expressing surprise or anxiety, and is short for 'Christ save our souls'. It was commonly used in the 1880s, by which time Queen Elizabeth had been lying speechless in her grave for more than 250 years.

'The most likely theory is that it was named after an Australian gentleman who did use to say 'Cripes!'

'In fact, his name was Eustace A Cripes.

'The story goes that around 1850 Eustace was up a creek without a paddle. He was looking for gold and he was lost, so he secured his boat to a tree and proceeded on foot. He immediately tripped over the diamond and fell flat on his face.

'Thinking he had literally stumbled across a worthless but

interesting lump of glass, and being very thirsty at the time, he sold it to a sheep farmer called Dan Under, in exchange for a billycan of beer.

'*Soon after, growing mentally unhinged by his fruitless search for gold, he killed himself with his own boomerang. He kept it as sharp as a razor, using it to shave his beard and chop up vegetables for stews. Apparently, after throwing the boomerang, Eustace chose not to duck when it came whizzing back at him. It did him a nasty mischief. He was buried the next day with his boomerang at his side.*

'*Thus the curse of the Fabulous Cripes Diamond was born.*'

'Ooh,' said Stella, her eyes opening wide with anticipation. 'Go on!'

'*According to the curse, whoever possesses the diamond is doomed to suffer a horrible death or a persistent streaming cold, whichever comes first.*

'*Sure enough, only a month after acquiring it, its new owner, Dan Under, 'handed in his tin plate', as the vulgar phrase has it, when he was savaged by one of his more irritable sheep.*

'*As Dan Under lay dying, covered in sheep bites, the diamond was stolen from beneath his bed by a lady friend called Rhoda Wallaby.*

'*Rhoda was a large-boned barmaid who sang uncouth but amusing songs in the local saloon bar, five hundred miles away. Ambitious to become a star on the London music hall stage, she sold the diamond to a one-legged gentleman who greatly admired her saucy songs. She immediately spent all the money on a one-way boat ticket to England.*

'*However, her dreams of fame and fortune were plagued by a mysterious streaming cold which wrecked her voice at every public engagement thereafter. Wheezing and croaking, she was booed off the boards time and again, till one sinister night she drowned in a bowl of water.*

'*Had she fainted while inhaling steam to unblock her nasal passages? Or was she murdered by a music lover driven insane by her ghastly singing? A Victorian fog of mystery surrounds the truth.*'

'How creepy,' giggled Stella, 'and yet gripping! Go on!'

Stirling Steele turned the page.

'*The Cripes Diamond's new owner was an Australian door-to-door carpet salesman called Walter Wall. He polished the diamond and used it as a decorative glass paperweight.*

'*Now, Walter was a man who could not resist a bet. If you said to him, 'I bet you a pint of beer you can't jump over that crocodile-infested stream,' he would say, 'You're on!'*

'*This explains, by the way, why he had only one leg, a fact that made his job so difficult, travelling from town to town carrying a heavy bag full of carpet samples.*

'*He was a friendly, optimistic type of bloke and was hoping to supply carpets for all the newly built prisons in Sydney – little realising how uncomfortable the cells were. But the Curse of the Cripes Diamond had other plans...*

'*The afternoon he arrived on the outskirts of Sydney, he stopped at an inn. The owner warned him, 'Whatever you do, don't go near the stream at the bottom of the back garden. It's full of man-eating crocodiles, and they're always hungry.'*

'*This gave Walter quite a turn and he made a mental note to keep well away from the stream.*

'*But that evening he had the misfortune (yes, the curse was working already!) to meet an English adventurer who had resolved to get his hands on Walter's meagre savings by fair means or foul.*

'*The gentleman called himself Lord Luke Downe, and he was a terrible liar. He was not, in fact, a lord of any realm at all, although he looked and sounded every inch the thoroughbred English aristocrat.*

'*His real name was Willie Cheetham and he hailed from a poor but honest family in Walthamstow. And he had no money, though he behaved as if he did, running up huge debts and then slipping away before he could be made to pay them.*

'*For example, he pretended that he was a close friend of Queen Victoria, which impressed everyone he met.*

'*He claimed he taught her to do cartwheels, but this was an outrageous fib. Like all rich ladies of that period, Queen Victoria wore cumbersome skirts called crinolines, which were hard enough to walk about in, never mind perform gymnastics!*

But people are very gullible and everybody he bumped into was delighted to lend him money, imagining their new acquaintance was on cartwheeling terms with Britain's reigning monarch. He would then cartwheel around the room – as if that proved anything!

'After drinking several glasses of local beer with Walter Wall, Lord Luke said, 'I say, Walter, come out into the jolly old back garden. I want to make you a bet.'

'Walter's curiosity was roused and he followed the bogus Lord, knocking over a chair and two stools with his bag containing bulky carpet samples and the paperweight.

'The sun was just beginning to go down and the red light made the eucalyptus trees shimmer like rubies.

"See those stepping stones out there?' Lord Luke pointed to the stream, which was flowing very quietly and innocently. Walter nodded.

"I bet you can't cross over to the other side on those stones without falling in.'

"How much do you bet me?' said Walter, unable to resist the thrill of a wager.

"Fifty dollars,' said Lord Luke.

"And what if I lose? How much do I pay you?'

"Oh nothing, old bean. I just enjoy a sporting bet. Oh wait a minute! I tell you what!' he said, pretending the thought had only just come to him. 'If you lose, you buy me a pint of beer.'

'Walter looked at the stream. There was no sign of a crocodile, only the dozen or so stepping stones forming a crooked path across the water.

"You're on!' he announced. They shook hands on it.

'Walter Wall was convinced that he would win because friends often said, 'For a man with one leg, you are remarkably graceful and agile.'

'However, Walter failed to notice that they only said this when he was in the bar offering to buy drinks for everyone.

"Walter, my dear fellow,' Lord Luke added in his politest manner, 'do let me guard your bag for you. It's clearly very heavy and might upset your balance.'

"Thank you, Lord Luke,' Walter replied, handing him his bag.

And off he set.

'Walter was half way across the stream when he stopped for a breather. The stepping stone on which he was standing opened one eye and looked up at him.

'There is an old proverb that says, 'Let sleeping dogs lie,' which obviously means try not to make unnecessary trouble for yourself. The same idea also applies to sleeping crocodiles.

'Sadly, Walter had contrived to make a great deal of trouble for himself. As he hobbled awkwardly towards the opposite bank, all the crocodiles woke up and proceeded to eat every scrap of him, including his wooden leg.

'Lord Luke promptly picked up the bag containing Walter's worldly goods – including the diamond – collected his own belongings and disappeared without a trace.

'And without paying his bill at the inn.'

Mr Steele stopped reading and looked at Stella.

'You've gone very quiet. Are you all right?'

'Yes,' Stella replied, paler than usual. 'I always go quiet when – when I sit in a chair.'

The truth was that the thought of being eaten alive by crocodiles had made her feel a bit queasy.

'Go on,' she urged.

'Lord Luke returned to London with all the money he had 'borrowed'. He claimed to be a brave explorer, recently returned from Mexico, where he had discovered a lost city called Fecha Picha.

'His plan was to sell this story to the newspapers for financial gain. However, little did he realise that a far more sinister fate awaited him – thanks to the Curse of the Cripes Diamond!'

Mr Steele paused again.

'Are you sure you want me to – '

'Yes,' Stella insisted emphatically. 'It's scary but I *must* know what comes next!'

'You're the boss.'

And Stirling Steele turned another page –

CHAPTER FOURTEEN

Royal Connections

– but Stella interrupted him before he could start again.

'If I had been Lord Luke, I would have gone straight to a jeweller's shop in London and had the rock valued.'

Mr Steele resumed reading.

'*Lord Luke went straight to a jeweller's shop in London and had the rock valued.*'

'Oh. Go on.'

'*The jeweller, Arthur Nicker, examined the rock through a magnifying glass. He knew at once that he was holding a huge diamond – one of enormous, maybe stupendous value.*

"*Yes, as I suspected. Just a worthless lump of quartz,' Arthur Nicker commented, because he was also a devious crook.*

"*Quite attractive in its own way, but of little value. I could sell it as a novelty doorstop, but it wouldn't fetch much. I'll give you five shillings for it.'*

"*An Oxford scholar, eh?' – his rhyming slang for a dollar.*

'*Lord Luke was tempted to accept the offer because he was always short of the readies – his term for cash. And the rock was proving a heavy nuisance to lug about.*

"*I'll think about it, old boy,' he said to the jeweller and, picking up his stolen property, he made for the door.*

'*Arthur Nicker was so horrified at losing a possibly vast fortune that he suffered an instant heart attack.*

"*Aagh... Baagh... Saagh...' he gasped, clutching his chest.*

"*Thank you, I will,' Lord Luke called out politely, thinking the jeweller had said, 'Come back soon, sir.'*

'*As Lord Luke closed the shop door behind him, the jeweller slumped to the floor, stone dead. Another victim of the curse of the Cripes Diamond.*

'Though disappointed that his rock was not precious, Lord Luke hoped it might be of some value while recounting his breathtaking and totally fictitious adventures.

'That very night, while drinking in a pub, he met a newspaper reporter from The Times by the name of Owen Deed.

"I say, Owen, this story might thrill your readers. I recently went to Mexico with several friends to look for lost cities. While climbing Mount Tappa-koppa-kettle, an earthquake caused a spectacular landslide. Countless tons of rocks cascaded down upon my companions, crushing them all to death. Miraculously, yours truly was unharmed, but it left me dangling at the end of a forty foot rope!

"The next day, I was still there – swinging helplessly to and fro. One is used to hanging around pubs in Soho but this was far worse. I badly needed to use the toilet!

"Occasionally a rock or two would fall near me, obliging me to twist my body into fantastical shapes to avoid being hit.

"Then an idea struck me! If I caught the next falling rock, it would increase my weight and break the rope, thus causing me to plummet – either to my death, down a bottomless chasm, or to my salvation if I landed in a tree.

"So I resolved to catch the next rock. Not as easy as catching the next bus! However, I remembered my cricket skills, honed on the playing fields of Eton. When the next blighter hurtled towards me, I lunged at it with almost superhuman strength.

"Howzat! I yelled, seizing the rock and hugging it to my chest.

"Snap! went the rope and down I dropped into the branches of a tree. Saved!

"Phew! What a lucky escape!'

'What a colossal fib.

"And here, my dear Owen, is the very rock that saved my life. I'm a sentimental old softie. I vowed on the spot never to part with it, even though it is just a dirty, shapeless lump. It reminds me of my dear mother.'

'Owen Deed did indeed print Lord Luke's story in The Times and nick-named him 'Lucky' Lord Luke.

'News of his gripping adventures soon reached the ears of none other than Queen Victoria, who invited Lucky Lord Luke to *tea at Buckingham Palace. His lie had come true! – except for the part about teaching her to do cartwheels.*

"Albert tells me you have had a dramatic brush with death. We should like to hear this colourful story.'

'She enjoyed a good yarn over a pot of Indian tea and a plate of Bath Oliver biscuits.

'He regaled the Queen with his hair-raising but totally fabricated tale.

"And this, ma'am, is the very rock that saved my life,' he announced, placing it on the table in front of Her Majesty.

"How interesting,' she said. 'My husband and I find mineralogy a fascinating field of study. Dear Albert is a positive mine of information on the subject. Consequently, we have assembled a large collection of rock samples. But we do not have one quite like this.'

'There was an uneasy pause in the conversation, in which Lord Luke felt that he was obliged to respond in an appropriate way. But he didn't.

"Yes,' Her Majesty continued, 'this rock-crystal would make an outstanding addition to our collection.'

'She nibbled a biscuit and waited.

"Then please accept it as a gift, your Majesty,' said Lord Luke, in a rather weak voice. 'I would consider it a great honour.'

"Most kind,' Her Majesty replied, placing the rock in a concealed pocket in her voluminous crinoline.

"More tea?'

'He was annoyed at losing his useful story-telling aid, but hoped his gesture might gain him access to some splendid, noble houses. Not to mention some splendid, noble wallets.

'Some weeks later, Prince Albert sent the rock away to be examined by experts at the British Museum.

'Their analysis was a model of accuracy and honesty:

> *"This rough, colourless diamond appears to be flawless. Properly cut, it would greatly exceed the weight and value of all other known diamonds many times.'*

'Prince Albert assumed it had been a generous gift to his dear wife from a wealthy but eccentric nobleman, and so he instructed

his secretary to write Lord Luke a charming letter of thanks.

'*However, the only forwarding address that Buckingham Palace had for Lord Luke was a seedy hotel in Spitalfields. A letter was duly posted.*

'*Within a few days the letter was returned. Attached to it was a note:*

"*Deer Royal Highness, I deeply regret to inform you that Lord Luke has legged it, leevin no forwardin' address. As manager of this here hotel, I wouldn't half be grateful to know the whereabouts of Lord Luke's currant hat rack, if his Royal Highness manages to dig it up.*

> Ever so sinceerly,
>
> Miles Cheaper'

'*The next day, there was an announcement in The Times:*

"*Her Majesty the Queen wishes to thank Lord Luke Downe for his priceless diamond. She presumes that Lord Luke has returned to Mexico to look for other lost cities. She hopes to thank him in person for his most generous gift when he returns to England.*'

'*However, immediately underneath this paragraph was a statement saying:*

"*London police are keen to arrest a man going about under the false name of Lord Luke Downe. He is strongly suspected of murdering a carpet salesman in Australia and not paying his hotel bill.*'

'*Lucky Lord Luke had finally run out of luck!*

'*He had squandered all his money – i.e. other people's – and he was on the run from the law.*

'*One miserably wet night, while sheltering under London Bridge, he was stuffing an old newspaper inside his leaky shoes when the article about the Queen's 'priceless diamond' caught his eye.*

'*He stared at it in shocked disbelief, realising he had given away a vast fortune! A trickle of rain ran down the back of his shivering neck, and his brain snapped.*

'*That night, passers-by were frightened by a scruffy tramp waving wet newspapers at them and babbling nonsense about being a fabulously rich lord.*

'*Soon after, according to a gossipy witness called Claire Voyant, he climbed onto one of the parapets of London Bridge and stood there 'laughing horribly'. Then he flung himself into the River Thames. Not for a swim.*

'*Willie Cheetham, the phoney Lord Downe, had once more vanished without trace – this time, permanently.*

'*The Curse of the Cripes Diamond had struck again!*'

'Another ghastly end!' announced Stella, quite satisfied with Lord Luke's watery fate.

'What happened to the diamond after that?'

'*And so Queen Victoria became the new owner. Was she stricken with the diamond's terrible curse?*

'*Well, within a few months, Prince Albert, her adored husband, fell prey to a killer disease called typhoid. His sudden death plunged the Queen into the deepest misery for the rest of her long life.*

'*She blamed his death on her son, Prince Edward.*

"*The way that nincompoop carries on would drive any father to an early grave! Gambling, parties and pretty ladies. That's all he thinks about. I can never look at him without a shudder.*'

'*And since then, Britain's royal family has suffered a series of painful scandals which it would be kinder not to list.*

'*Years passed, and the diamond lay forgotten inside a locked cupboard in Buckingham Palace under a constantly mounting pile of objects.*

'*Each day, adoring subjects bombarded the monarch with presents of every kind – from ruby tiaras to teddy bears, from antique medallions to moleskin muffs. Gold clocks, silver cups, leopard skin cloaks and bronze busts.*

'*In 1924, the entire haul was carted off to King George V's Private Collection in Windsor Castle. By this time, nobody had the faintest idea what the odd-looking lump of glass at the bottom of the heap was.*

"*Ah! The very thing I need in this hot weather!*' cried the curator, Tudor Beams. '*A doorstop.*' *And he placed it on the floor to keep a breeze blowing through his office – following Arthur Nicker's devious suggestion precisely!*

'However, it soon attracted the attention of a weak-chinned guardsman called Captain Aemon Farr, who stubbed his polished boot on it.

"What is that wretched object?!' he shouted.

'No one seemed to know. Or care.

'After a bit of sly detective work, he was very pleasantly surprised to discover how much the doorstop was really worth.

'For several months, he had been eyeing the Private Collection for a costly trinket to 'half inch'.

'And so, one sunny morning, while Mr Beams was 'paying a visit', Captain Farr popped the diamond inside his tall busby, marched smartly back to barracks and hid it under his bed.

'That afternoon, a draught swept through Mr Beams' office and slammed his door shut. The loud bang made him jump, tipping a bottle of royal blue ink all over his desk.

"Drat. Where's my doorstop gone?' he muttered.

'Mildly curious to know exactly what the stone was, he climbed a ladder to the top of a tall, dusty bookcase and consulted his files. He was horrified by what he read. His shocking loss of such a valuable asset would certainly cost him his job – if he reported it missing.

'Dear me. This must be kept quiet,' he thought.

'His fingers trembled as he hastily replaced the file. He began to descend, dropped his spectacles and started shaking from head to foot. He then lost his balance and fell off the ladder, pulling the entire bookcase down on top of him.

'Almost every bone in his body was crushed. Six months later, he died in pitiful agony – without confessing his costly mistake.

'The theft remained unspotted for years, by which time Captain Farr had sailed away with the diamond to America.

'There, he sold it secretly for cash to a Russian billionaire.

'The buyer, Ivan Akinkoff, had the stone cut and polished by a jeweller called Gore Blimey. The result was a spectacular success – the biggest and most dazzlingly beautiful diamond in the world!

'It was set on a gold chain and the billionaire gave it to his *wife to wear around her neck for a very unusual occasion.*

'*But what happened to the weak-chinned Captain Farr? – I hear you ask.*'

'Yes, what?!' cried Stella. 'Did he come a horrible cropper as well?'

'*All his life, Captain Farr had been ashamed of his puny chin and longed for a square, manly jaw to jut proudly over his chest. So he spent all his ill-gotten money on plastic surgery carried out at the Rudy Mentry Beauty Clinic in Los Angeles.*

'*However, the operations went hideously wrong.*

'*First, his chin stuck out to the left. Then it stuck out to the right. Finally, after twelve painful procedures, his jaw was so big and heavy, he had to strap it up with a leather belt.*

"*I feel such a fool,' he complained through clenched teeth to anyone who could be bothered to listen – even complete strangers at bus stops. But they looked back at him blankly, because his jaw was so big and the strap so tight, no one could understand a word he was saying.*'

'How did the guardsman die? Was it a streaming cold this time?' Stella asked, grinning with ghoulish interest.

'Funny you should say that,' Stirling Steele answered, glancing at what came next.

'*Captain Farr's fate is almost too terrible to relate.*'

'Go on!' she insisted, with a scared giggle.

CHAPTER FIFTEEN

Lethal Ice

'I can't go on,' Stirling Steele said.

'Why? Are you fed up?'

'No, I feel great. But it says here –
>   'WARNING
>   *The following account is*
>   *UNSUITABLE FOR CHILDREN.*"

'I am not children,' Stella pointed out coolly. 'Keep reading.'

'Captain Farr caught a filthy cold that went to his head, as colds do, and it got worse and worse, till he could barely breathe through his nose. That evening, he strapped up his huge chin extra tight, to stop himself falling out of bed. He was determined to get a good night's sleep.

'As he lay there in the early hours he gave a sudden, violent sneeze. Bang! The force of the sneeze exploded like a bomb inside his head. The plastic surgery stitches split open and his face burst completely apart.

'Neighbours reported the noise to the police. The next morning his body was discovered.

'Chief Officer Dick Tater said, "That stiff was a total mess. I ain't never seen nothin' like it. Poor sucker was all over the place."

'The coroner, Cherrie Picker, pronounced the Cause of Death as chronic sternutation.

'Yeah,' commented Chief Officer Tater. 'Fancy label for one helluva sneeze. I suspected foul play, but it looks like the guy just went completely to pieces.'

Stella picked up the phone next to her armrest. 'Are we nearly there yet?'

'Not long now, Miss Wishbone.'

'Do you want me to stop?' asked Stirling Steele.

'Oh no! Tell me what happened to the Russian billionaire,' Stella asked, gloating over the carnage.

'Ivan Akinkoff was married to a glamorous American ice-skater called Lee Nova. He worshipped the ice she skidded about on and, determined to make her an international star, he produced ice spectaculars for her to appear in.

"Our next show will be something amazing! Sensational! At end you will dance knock-out solo number wearing this diamond round your neck!'

'He billed her as –

The Greatest Ice-Skater In The World.

*'There was only one snag. She was **not** the greatest ice-skater in the world. In fact, she kept falling over. And she was well aware of the fact.*

"Ivan, sweetheart, I beg you. Please don't make me do this. I'm a lousy skater! Everyone knows it except you. I stink! My backside is black and blue!'

"Who say this, my pretty icicle? You are marvellous skater,' Ivan reassured her. 'So what if you slip up now and then? The customers don't even notice. They think is all part of the routine.'

"They notice all right. They boo me. It's OK for you. You don't have to take it.'

'A fierce Russian rage darkened his features.

"Listen! If wasn't for me, you still be working in filthy sack factory! You do what I tell you! End of discussion!'

'Lee Nova lived in fear of her husband's volcanic temper, so she meekly agreed, and worked even harder on her spins and jumps. But alas, practice did not make perfect.

'During the rehearsals, Ivan constantly interfered with colourful but time-wasting comments.

"Your final number will be terrific! Imagine the scene – A Siberian forest at night. Is winter. Stars are twinkling. You shoot onto ice dressed as snowflake, wearing your fabulous diamond. You look enchanting as you leap and lunge and whiz round and round, like you was caught in swirling snowstorm. Your beauty and skill dazzle everyone. And so does your sparkler!'

'This sounded fine in theory, but he was forgetting one important thing. The Cripes Diamond is almost the size of a rugby football, which makes it very cumbersome.

'An ice-dancing champion called Vera Way was paid to choreograph the routine. She strongly advised Lee not to wear the jewel round her neck.

"It's a loose cannon. And almost as heavy as a real one! Believe me, it'll wreck your sense of balance.'

"No! She'll get used to it!' Ivan yelled. 'The rock stays in the number! End of discussion!'

'At the first performance in Chicago, Lee Nova leapt onto the ice for the closing number. The tinsel spikes sticking out of her elbows and shoulders made her look more like a hedgehog than a snowflake.

'The glittering diamond swung uncontrollably from her slender neck, causing her to teeter and topple in an ungainly fashion. But Lee Nova pretended it was all part of the helpless snowflake's haphazard dance in the wind. She fell flat on her face several times – and also on her 'clumsy ass', as one spectator put it.

'She executed the final spin. The snowstorm music grew louder and louder. Faster and faster the snowflake twirled. Tighter and tighter the chain wrapped itself around her throat and, as clouds of blue smoke engulfed her, she crashed onto the ice.

'Blackout. Silence.

'An awkward pause.

'At this point, Lee Nova was supposed to glide forward gracefully out of the smoke on one leg, her arms raised to receive wild cheers and applause. But no Lee Nova. And no wild applause. Except from her wild husband.

'The clouds finally cleared. Gasps of horror. Screams.

'Poor Lee Nova, her neck broken, was revealed lying crumpled on the ice, beyond help. Her spirit had skated up to that great ice-rink in the sky.

'The Cripes Diamond had claimed another life!'

'Are we nearly there yet?' Stella asked the pilot again.

'Not long now, Miss Wishbone.'

'Did the billionaire die as well?'

'*Alone in his vast, dark mansion, Ivan Akinkoff sobbed as he locked the doom-laden diamond inside his safe. He was so heartbroken, he vowed he would never speak to another living soul again! Or cut his hair, or trim his fingernails or toenails.*

'*And so he lived the rest of his life as a strange, unwashed hermit, leaving scrawled notes everywhere instructing his servants to mend his spectacles or change a light bulb.*

'*He smelt so awful and looked so weird, they were only too glad not to approach him.*

'*And there inside his safe the diamond remained, till a safe-cracker called Brian Large, decided to steal it.*

'*Brian was a boastful thief with a huge mouth. As a party trick, he would place an apple, an orange and a banana in his mouth and then shut it as if there was nothing inside!*

'*His plan was to disguise himself as a window-cleaner, break into the millionaire's study, unlock the safe, remove the diamond and hide it inside his enormous mouth.*

'*He would then stroll innocently away from the scene of the crime with his ladder over his shoulder, puckering his lips as if he were whistling a quiet tune to himself.*

'*All went as planned, except that Brian happened to trip over the end of his ladder while crossing the lawn. He gulped and half-swallowed the diamond which lodged in his throat and choked him to death.*

'*When his girlfriend, Dianna Sorr, was told how he had died, her only comment was, "Him and his big mouth! I knew it would get him into trouble one day."*

'*The diamond was extracted from Brian, thoroughly washed and popped back in the safe.*'

'But the Russian billionaire! What happened to him?' Stella asked impatiently.

'*Ivan Akinkoff's death was the weirdest of all.*

'*He had Lee Nova's body deep-frozen in his basement. She was preserved standing up in a glass tank, wearing her skating outfit and smiling cheerfully. On ice for ever.*

'*At night, he would visit his wife and talk to her through the window. Sometimes he wept and begged her forgiveness. '"Lee! I did it all for you!" he wailed. "For you!"*

'At other times he screamed, 'You stupid, knock-kneed, frostbitten knucklehead! You lazy, ungrateful idiot!'

'And her unblinking eyes would stare back at him silently.

'Oddly, his wild grief did not affect his business cunning. He studied up-to-the-minute financial reports, and one day, without warning anyone, he cashed in all his stocks and bonds. They were worth billions of dollars. The panic which this instantly spread was thought to have caused the great Wall Street crash of 1929. He then reinvested his money and doubled his fortune on the loss of others.

'Years passed, and his beard, hair and nails grew longer and longer till he looked like a forest creature.

'Then one day a stranger sent him something that brought an abrupt end to this existence. It was a copy of a book called How To Live Forever. In it the author, Lester Cartround, made this curious claim: 'Eating food is a disgusting habit. The purest thing you can live on is air.'

'This idea inspired Ivan Akinkoff to write a bizarre will.

"Air has been scientifically proved to be the most nourishing food of all. People are crazy to sit around shoving that other filthy stuff in their faces. Beetroots grow in dirt! Ugh! From now on, I eat nothing but air.

"When I die, which is most likely never, I want my body to be frozen and placed alongside my beloved wife's. Then NASA will transport the two of us to Mars in SkySkater One, a spacecraft specially designed for the purpose.

"Scientists on Mars are way ahead of ours. Using their advanced knowledge, they will un-freeze our bodies and bring us back to eternal life. I will then make Lee the greatest dancer on ice in the entire universe – as she was destined to be. This is my solemn and final wish.

"Signed – Ivan Akinkoff.'

'Three weeks later, a servant sniffed out his remains. He had been dead for several days.

'*It was never discovered who sent him the book. Many people would like to thank the person.*

'*Ivan's will was strictly followed. All his worldly goods were sold – including the Cripes Diamond. The sale raised billions of dollars, and Ivan and his wife, frozen solid, were duly blasted off to the red planet in SkySkater One.*

'*Nine months later the rocket developed a fault, swerved off course and hurtled past Mars at half a mile a second.*

'*A top team at NASA's Mission Control was tracking its progress on a computer screen. They looked at one another.*

'*The supervisor, Oliver Sudhan, said, 'Oh well, that's that. Who's for coffee?'*

'*SkySkater One has now left our galaxy. In a few million years it will reach the far edge of the universe and then continue travelling beyond it, probably for all eternity.*'

Stella was transfixed by this unearthly vision.

'So they're flying through space. Right now.'

'Guess so,' Stirling Steele replied.

'Frozen solid.'

'Yeah.'

'Creepy.'

Stella gulped and quickly picked up the phone.

'Are we nearly there yet?'

'Not long now, Miss.'

Stirling Steele looked concerned. 'Had enough?'

Stella shook her head determinedly.

'I've got to know what happened next. Who bought the diamond?'

'*Which brings us to the present day. The last person to buy the Cripes Diamond was a very elderly American businessman by the name of Andy Tipoff, who amassed a vast fortune from ACNE.*'

'The skin complaint?' Stella enquired, puzzled.

'*ACNE stands for Amalgamated CocoNut Enterprises.*'

'Oh! I see – an acronym,' she observed, correctly. 'But how does anyone get rich from coconuts?'

'*The white coconut lining is delicious to eat fresh or dried. But that is just the beginning!*

'The shell and fibres can be turned into matting and ropes, and its oil extracts used to make soap, margarine, salad dressings, cosmetics, ointments and candles. The residue is used in cattle feed.

'People wondered why Andy Tipoff bought the Cripes Diamond.

"Because I can,' he had boasted.

'From that moment, serious health problems plagued the ancient wheeler-dealer and he spent months at a time on life-support machines.

'When questioned about the diamond's infamous curse, Andy's response was always the same – a dry chuckle, usually followed by a choking fit.

"Curse?' he would finally ask, leaning against the nearest wall and gasping for breath. 'What curse?'

'On his 99th birthday, he married a 22-year-old Californian model called Patty O'Dawes.

'His wedding present to his bride? – the Cripes Diamond!

'The next day, while honeymooning on his private island in the Bahamas, he was sitting under a palm tree chatting to her when a coconut fell on his head and killed him instantly.

'His young widow has never been able to describe his death without laughing uncontrollably.

'When a friend remarked, 'That must've been some tough nut,' Patty had replied, 'Yeah, but he was kinda cute. I'll miss the old guy.'

'Mr Tipoff left a complicated will. In it, his fortune is divided equally between Patty, his seven ex-wives and his sixteen children. This document has mysteriously disappeared.

'Patty claims that all the money should go to her but the other wives are taking the matter to court. Legal actions could drag on for years.

'Until it is settled, no one is allowed to touch a penny of his massive fortune. This has led to divorce, suicide and gross obesity problems.

'Since becoming the diamond's new owner, Patty has also suffered some grisly mishaps.

'A new central heating boiler blew up and threw her through

the kitchen window. As she lay on the lawn screaming, her pet poodle became excited, rushed over to Patty and bit off the end of her nose. It was sewn back later.

'*After recovering in hospital, Patty treated herself to a relaxing, candle-lit bath, fell asleep and set fire to her head.*

'*And so the curse continues...*

"*I am selling that rock,' Patty O'Dawes recently said, 'to keep what's left of my body and soul together.'*

'*Tomorrow in Vienna, the world's super-rich gather to bid for this deadly diamond.*

Who will be the next owner? Or victim...
THE END'

At that moment, the phone by Stella's elbow buzzed. It was the pilot's relaxing voice.

'Vienna air control have given us permission to land, Miss Wishbone.'

'Let's do it!' Stella shouted merrily.

'How are you feeling now?' Stirling Steele asked.

'Much better!'

'Hasn't this article worried you a bit?'

'No. Firstly, because I don't believe in curses. And secondly, I don't believe anything I read in the papers.'

This remark struck Mr Steele as particularly odd.

Stella had believed every word of the newspaper report about her mother. It had proved all too true. Hence her furious reaction. But she would use any argument to prove a case.

'They make up lies and rubbish just to sell thousands of papers. Look!'

She snatched the magazine from Stirling Steele.

'This article – some of it doesn't make any sense!' she complained. 'For example, this part. How did the writer know that Ivan Akinkoff cried when he locked the diamond in his safe? He was all alone. It said so.'

'Maybe he told someone that he cried.'

'He never spoke to anyone again! I think somebody made the whole thing up.'

She had a point.

'Anyhow, they were such stupid people. *That* was their curse! I'm more intelligent than the entire lot put together.'

She wasn't boasting. She meant it quite sincerely.

'So I really have cheered you up?'

'Totally!'

Stella looked out of the window excitedly, as the plane descended into the white clouds.

'All I need now is the Cripes Diamond and your birthday present, and I shall be the happiest girl in the world! And the richest!'

Or so she thought.

END OF PART ONE

PART TWO

CHAPTER SIXTEEN

First the Bad News

The next morning, Stella went to an expensive shop in Vienna and bought a new bag. It was bright green.

When she returned to the hotel, Mr Steele was having breakfast.

'Happy birthday!' he said. 'Here's your present!'

He placed a box on the table.

'I bet you can't guess what it is.'

'Give me a clue.'

'Think of a famous composer who lived in Vienna.'

'I can't!' Stella answered impatiently, untying the ribbon.

'Is it something to wear?'

Mr Steele smiled. 'No.'

'Is it something to eat?'

'No, but you're getting warmer.'

She tore off the gold wrapping paper.

'I bet I know what it is! It's – '

She opened the box.

'Beethoven,' she said, a little disappointed.

A marble head of the great composer frowned at her. She knew it was Beethoven because his name was printed along the base.

'He looks ever so grumpy,' she observed.

'Well, he went deaf when he was thirty, according to the shop chappie. That might have had something to do with it. He kept smashing up pianos because he thumped them harder and harder, trying to hear what he was playing. Do you like it?'

'Of course I do. I shall put it on my desk and every time I look at it I shall think of – ' she hesitated and bit her lower lip, shyly – 'of Beethoven.'

And she put the bust in her new green bag.

'Look. He fits perfectly!'

Mr Steele stood up. 'We'd better get cracking. The auction starts in half an hour.'

As Stella and her personal secretary were driven to the grand auction in Vienna, she remembered the advice her father had once given her about bidding for something in an auction sale.

*'Before the auction begins, first work out the top price you are prepared to pay. Then, you write that amount on a bit of paper. If the bidding goes above your price, you tear the paper up and walk out. Never, **never** be tempted to go **above** the price you decided on.'*

Stella worked out her price.

On a piece of paper she wrote – Eighty million pounds. She always knew how much she was worth, down to the last penny, and she decided that eighty million was as much as she could reasonably afford. A tidy sum. And this was a few years ago when a million pounds was worth something.

But would it be enough to bag the Fabulous Cripes Diamond?

All her financial advisers had thrown their hands up in horror, begging her not to take the risk.

But she was determined.

'I want that diamond,' she had shouted at them, 'and I am going to get it! And what's more, you're all fired!' she had yelled as she marched out.

The sale was held in a splendid palace.

As cool as a cucumber, Stella climbed out of her car and marched up the steps to the ornate entrance hall, where staggeringly rich people were milling about.

Oddly enough, they didn't appear to be particularly wealthy. In fact, one man was wearing a faded T-shirt and a grubby pair of jeans with rips across his knees. But she soon realised this was a statement.

'I'm so rich, I don't need to look *as if I am!'*

She entered the ballroom, which was lit by crystal chandeliers. Over the years, countless well-off feet had waltzed across that marble floor. But today it was transformed into a magnificent auction room. Rows of elegant but uncomfortable chairs had been set out facing a stage at the far end.

Millionaires of assorted shapes and sizes had flown to Vienna from all seven continents to take part. Some had been unable to attend in person because they were too lazy, too busy, or too ill. One was even on his deathbed yet desperate to own the diamond! These millionaires had sent trusty aides to bid on their behalf, keeping in contact every second by phone.

Stella sat on a gilt chair, clutching her piece of paper, her legs dangling.

The international press was present in full force – buzz, buzz, buzz – like wasps round a pot of raspberry jam. They had a wonderful view of the proceedings, watching from a gallery where musicians usually played jolly dance music. Each reporter was waiting to reveal the name of the dangerous diamond's new owner.

The noisy chatter reminded her of a flock of birds.

Birds! Her thoughts flew back to poor little Sandy Bottom lying alone in his hospital bed, and his mother's appeal to her...

'He keeps asking when you'll come and see him again.'

Now, surrounded by so much wealth, she felt very mean.

'I was horrid not to visit him. He needed cheering up,' she thought guiltily.

And she remembered their run-down house with its broken front gate, the handsome book Sandy had generously given her and how much she had enjoyed his company.

'Well, at least he's got a parrot to amuse him,' she said to herself, still slightly jealous. Then she shook the picture of him out of her head.

The next moment, all chattering stopped.

Everyone's attention turned to a silver-haired gentleman in an elegant suit who had appeared on the stage.

He was the auctioneer.

He bowed charmingly to the rich assembly.

'Good afternoon,' he said, in several languages. 'My name is Watson Opalworth. On behalf of ACNE, it gives me great pleasure to welcome you to this historic sale.'

There was a polite pit-a-pat of applause. Rich people don't clap very loudly. They usually pay other people to do it for them. But things were to change – as we shall see.

'And so without further ado,' Mr Opalworth continued, 'let us turn to the business in hand. Ladies and gentlemen – the Fabulous Cripes Diamond!'

He made a dramatic gesture with both his arms to the centre of the stage. An ear-splitting blast of trumpets echoed through the hall and made everyone nearly fall off their chairs.

A brilliant spotlight shone on what looked like a puppet theatre placed on a fancy table. Its crimson velvet curtains parted – and there was the Fabulous Cripes Diamond!

Gasps of amazement escaped from the audience.

It was even bigger and more spectacular than anyone had imagined from its photographs – a fantastic, mouth-watering vision.

The dazzling jewel slowly revolved on a plush turntable, sending splinters of multicoloured lights zigzagging all over the gilded walls and ceiling. Gasps turned to applause, then to cheers, then to a standing ovation, as if they were welcoming a celebrity footballer. Once again, this lump of carbon's irresistible fascination had worked its magic spell!

At that moment, every millionaire in the hall was desperate to own the diamond, whatever the cost.

Stella had caught a mere glimpse through the wall of wealthy backs blocking her view. But that was enough. Her fingers tightened around her piece of paper.

The commotion didn't subside; it grew louder.

Some people fainted from sheer excitement and had to be woken up by Red Cross nurses. Others burst into tears of pleasure. Or greed. Or both.

Violent quarrels broke out as passions flared. One man hit another man's nose.

There were loud shouts. 'I *shall* have it!'

'No you *won't*, you fat ugly grub!'

'Yes I *will!*'

Mr Opalworth was secretly pleased by this reaction. He knew the price would go sky high.

'Please remain calm,' he appealed.

A sudden silence came over the room. Everyone stopped being silly, sat straight in their chairs and folded their hands neatly in their laps.

'I shall now start the auction,' he announced with quiet authority. 'Who will kindly open the bidding at – shall we say – one million pounds?'

Arms flew up in the air and the race was on.

He pointed to a man waving a peacock's feather.

'Thank you, sir. I have a bid for one million pounds from the gentleman at the back with the large plume. Am I bid one and a half million?' he asked, in a voice as rich as a dark chocolate biscuit.

Hands shot up again and so did the price. It jumped. It leapt. It soared.

Up and up and up and up!

And up and up and up and up!

The minutes whizzed by like Frisbees as the price rocketed beyond all expectations – way above Stella's eighty million pounds limit. She looked down at the piece of paper in her hand, breathless with anger. Or greed. Or both.

'It's incredible!' the TV news reporters babbled. 'It beggars belief! Eighty-four million pounds and still rising!'

However, half an hour later, a strange hush had fallen over the proceedings. The bidding had reached the mind-boggling price of ninety-eight and a half million pounds!

And only two people were still bidding.

One was a neat little Japanese lady, by the name of Kim Ono. She was the boss of a cosmetics empire – a delicate but ruthless beauty.

She raised her silver fan.

'I am bid ninety-nine million pounds by Madame Ono.'

Everybody exclaimed in astonishment. One man screamed like a girl and then cleared his throat as if it was a mistake.

'Any advance on that price?'

All eyes swerved to the other bidder. He was a chubby Greek called Costa Pakit, who was sitting very calmly, not far from Stella – a stinking-rich owner of dirty great oil tankers.

The auctioneer waited for his reaction. Mr Pakit simply lowered his left eyelid a quarter of an inch. This was his curious way of bidding, hard to spot by anyone but the auctioneer.

'Ninety-nine and a half million pounds I am bid,' said Mr Opalworth smoothly, with a discreet nod of his head to the Greek. He then turned his eyes to Madame Ono. And waited.

There followed a heart-stopping silence.

Madam Ono was seated in the front row. She was staring straight at the Cripes Diamond.

If she had been carved out of ice, she could not have been more still. What was she thinking?

The pause seemed to last for ever. No one dared to breathe, never mind scratch an armpit.

Suddenly, she smacked her fan shut with a sharp *crack*, making everyone jump. She *snapped* open her bag, placed the fan inside, and closed the clasp with a loud *click*.

She stood up, smiled coldly at the auctioneer and gave him a gracious bow. She then turned her back on him and began to walk away down the centre aisle.

As everyone watched her sensational exit, her high-heeled shoes echoed like pistol shots in the marble hall. *Tap-tap-tap*.

Did this mean that Mr Pakit was about to be the new owner of the Fabulous Cripes Diamond? He grinned broadly, revealing a mouthful of large gold teeth.

'The price is now ninety-nine and a half million pounds, ladies and gentlemen. Do we have any more bids?'

Silence.

'Any more bids? One hundred million perhaps? No? For the last time, going to the person who wishes to remain anonymous – dressed in a bright yellow jacket in the third row with silver hair and a dark tan.'

Another deathly silence.

'Going once.'

Not a sound.

'Going twice.'

The auctioneer raised his gavel.

He opened his mouth to speak.

'One hundred million pounds and forty-eight pence!' called

out a small but clear voice.

Bewildered faces turned in every direction. No one could fathom where the voice had come from. Murmur-murmur.

'Are my ears going funny?'

'It sounded like a budgerigar.'

'Is someone playing the giddy goat?'

'What are pence?'

Mr Opalworth raked the hall with his sharp blue eyes.

'Would the person who made the last bid kindly offer some sort of identification? By raising a hand, perhaps?'

Stella did as she was asked, but the tips of her fingers barely broke the surface of puzzled heads. So, with Mr Steele's assistance, she clambered onto the seat of her chair.

'It's me, Stella Wishbone!' she declared. 'I bid one hundred million pounds, and forty-eight pence! Take it or leave it!'

There was a tremendous gasp from everyone.

'This is outrageous!'

'Who let that child in here?'

'She should be in bed!'

'It's a ventriloquist's dummy.'

But it was true.

Stella had become infected with the Cripes Diamond fever.

She was bidding far above the price she had decided on. Her entire fortune!

One glimpse of the spectacular gem and forgotten was all her father's valuable advice. And so was her piece of paper.

The torn up shreds lay underneath her chair.

Her heart was pounding; her eyes were staring; she felt dizzy with excitement. Only one thing mattered. She *had* to have the Cripes Diamond, whatever the cost.

It was, as her Aunt Zany would have said, sheer madness!

Stirling Steele smiled at Stella. His mouth gaped, like a shark about to gobble up a tasty kipper.

CHAPTER SEVENTEEN

And Now for the *Really* Bad News

'I am bid one hundred million pounds – and forty-eight pence.'

The hall echoed with feverish chattering...

'Who is this person?'

'No idea.'

'A mere chit of a girl!'

'What's a chit?'

'Quiet, please. Quiet,' Mr Opalworth pleaded.

Complete silence.

'Thank you. Any advance on that offer, ladies and gentlemen?'

The auctioneer's cool gaze rested on the Greek tycoon. But Mr Pakit's left eyelid remained motionless.

'Going once.' Mr Opalworth paused.

'Going twice!'

Everyone waited breathlessly to see what Mr Pakit would do.

Turning his face slowly, he gave Stella a wicked smile, baring his big gold teeth. He then shook his head.

'You win,' he murmured. 'It's yours.'

BANG! went the auctioneer's gavel.

'*Sold!* – for one hundred million pounds and forty-eight pence, to the young lady standing on the chair.'

For a moment, the entire gathering sat in transfixed silence, unable to believe what had happened. But they quickly recovered from the initial shock and rewarded Stella with a sitting ovation.

It was certainly more seemly than the earlier uproar. Even so, many disapproved of this unusual turn of events.

A small child had snatched the famous prize from right under their noses!

One lady from Brazil protested loudly.

'This can't be legal. My goldfish is older than she is!'

However, if you have a hundred million pounds to spend, it seems you can do pretty much what you like.

Television cameras beamed Stella's rather dazed expression around the world as reporters announced the sensational result.

'The Fabulous Cripes Diamond always comes up with a surprise. We know that. But who expected such a dramatic finish to this sale?!'

'Sell everything!'

Stella was hot on the phone to her finance manager – the only one she hadn't sacked. Skip Bale couldn't believe his ears.

'By everything, do you mean – everything?'

'That's right. The house, the planes, the factories, sell the entire lot – down to the last fork and spoon! I have to sign a cheque for one hundred million pounds and forty-eight pence tonight!'

And so Mr Bale did exactly as she demanded. Everything was sold. Even her favourite hot water bottle. Her dream had become a reality! The Fabulous Cripes Diamond was hers at last.

But would she inherit the curse as well?

Climbing into her posh hotel bed that night, Stella felt as if she owned the entire world. She can't have made a mistake. Millionaires had praised her...

'You beat me to it.'

'Smart operator, kid.'

'Great job.'

'Let's do lunch.'

And her thoughts were just as grand as her bed...

'I wonder if Buckingham Palace will make me a Dame...'

For doing what, precisely, she was too weary to imagine, but as she drifted off, the idea greatly appealed to her.

Dame Stella Wishbone had an impressive ring to it.

However, the following morning she woke up with a nasty bump. Her confidence had vanished like smoke up a chimney, and she faced the alarming truth of her situation. She owned nothing in the world now, except a sparkling rock!

Elaborate security arrangements had been worked out for transporting the Cripes Diamond back to England.

It was locked in a steel box. Stella had the only key. During the return flight, the box was attached to the table in front of her by seven chains secured by seven thick bolts.

Sitting down next to her, Mr Steele said, 'That was *really* clever! You must be feeling *fantastic!'*

However, a muted 'Mmm' was all Stella could manage.

'So, now you've actually bought the actual diamond, how much actual money have actually you got left?'

'Not much,' she answered evasively. 'But I can borrow plenty to live on until I sell the diamond next year.'

'Brilliant! A terrific investment. I think you're *really* clever!'

She secretly wished he would stop telling her how clever she was. It made her feel strangely nervous.

Her pilot buzzed her.

'Miss Wishbone. We'll be landing shortly at London City Airport. The weather in England is very cold with heavy snow forecast.'

'Right. Give me a minute to go to the toilet,' she said, and hung up. 'I've just spent millions. Now I've got to spend a penny!'

'Excellent!' Stirling Steele snorted with laughter. 'You're really clever!'

Stella winced and popped into the ladies.

Ten minutes later, the pink plane began its slow dive into the snow-thick clouds. Its new owner, a false teeth manufacturer called Constance Pitting was waiting on the runway to take possession the moment it landed.

The British press had gathered to welcome Stella in the reception lounge. Every newspaper, magazine and TV channel wanted shots of her wearing the Cripes Diamond round her neck, if she could bear its weight!

The steel box was wheeled in by security guards and placed on a table. Stella entered to great cheers, followed by Mr Steele, carrying her green bag.

Again, Stella had to stand on a chair to be seen by all.

A microphone was placed in front of her.

Flash, flash, flash! went the cameras. Stella put on her dark glasses and smiled, like a movie star.

Reporters yelled every kind of question at her.

'How does it feel to own the Cripes Diamond, Stella?'

'Are you planning to write an autobiography?'

'Host a TV chat show?'

'Record a pop album?'

'Manage a football club?'

'Ladies and gentlemen, I haven't changed. I am still the same ordinary, humble, down-to-earth person I always was.' She shrugged. 'A simple girl who enjoys simple things. I just happen to own the biggest diamond in the whole world, that's all. And the most expensive,' she pointed out.

'Don't keep us waiting, Stella! Let's see the rock!'

'With great pleasure.'

She produced the key from her pocket, inserted it into the lock and turned it three times.

Click. Click. Click.

'Ladies and gentlemen – '

Stella looked at the crowd, eager to witness their utter astonishment the moment the diamond was revealed.

'I present to you – '

She paused dramatically.

' – the Fabulous Cripes Diamond!'

And she whipped open the door of the steel box.

There was a stunned silence.

Every face was staring at its contents with a baffled expression. Not the reaction she had expected.

'Here it is, everybody!'

She pointed to the box for added emphasis.

'This is – '

'Beethoven,' someone said.

'No. It's – '

She glanced inside and found herself staring straight at the composer's famous frown.

'Beethoven,' she repeated flatly.

There was an awkward pause.

Stella removed her dark glasses and peered closer. It had to be a weird trick of the light.

The crowd waited for her to explain.

'No. It can't be Beethoven,' she insisted. 'Beethoven is in my bag. Hold on a second.'

She turned to Stirling Steele.

'Stir, give me my green bag.'

Another uncomfortable silence.

Because there was no green bag.

Because there was no Stir.

And there was no Fabulous Cripes Diamond.

Someone screamed loudly. Stella was shocked by the awful noise, and then realised it was coming from her own mouth.

The rest of the day passed in a blur of questions.

She was vaguely aware of getting into a police car... of snow falling... of arriving home... of being met by Mr Beeswax... the annoying solicitor...

'Go to bed,' he advised. 'I shall sort everything out for you. We'll talk in the morning.'

She woke the next day thinking, 'What a stupid dream. All muddled up and ridiculous. Things don't disappear into thin air.'

She opened her eyes and wiggled her toes. It felt wonderful to be home again, safe and sound. She sat up.

The room was unusually chilly.

Outside the window, her garden lay snoozing under a thick quilt of snow.

Complete silence.

'Snow makes everything so quiet!'

Too quiet. Something was wrong.

'What's the time?' No clock.

'What's on the business channel?' No TV.

'Where's my breakfast?!' she shouted. No answer.

She phoned the maid's room. Nothing.

She tried all the other extension numbers. No reply.

No maid. No cook. No housekeeper. No butler. No bodyguards. No chauffeur. No one. The house was empty.

And something else was missing. But what?

She glanced all round the room. What was different? She ended up staring at the far corner. Her heart gave a jump.

No yellow cello. Even that had gone.

There was a knock at the door.

'Come in!' she called out.

Panic over. Breakfast at last. Or maybe Aunt Zany. Yes, it was sure to be Aunt Zany!

The door opened and she beheld Mr Beeswax's stern, bespectacled face.

'Good morning, Stella. Did you sleep well?'

'Oh, it's you. Tell my maid I want breakfast. Now!'

'All your servants have gone.'

'They'd better get back or I'll fire them!'

'You already did. Don't you remember?'

Stella stared at him blankly, as if he had just told her that the Prime Minister of Britain was a teapot.

A few minutes later, she was sipping a glass of orange juice in the kitchen.

Mr Beeswax sat down in a chair opposite her.

'Where shall I begin? First, it is my unpleasant duty to inform you that the new owner wishes to move in this afternoon.'

Stella gazed oddly at the snow outside the window.

'I'll fly to Switzerland today. Tell my pilot to get the blue plane ready.'

'Stella, you sold both your planes. You sold everything, including this house, every stick of furniture and all fixtures and fittings, down to the last fork and spoon. Those were your specific orders. The new owner, Juno Wott, wants you out by two o'clock.'

Mr Beeswax tried to explain the gravity of the situation. It was an uphill task.

'You see, Stella, a child with no parents and nowhere to live is made something called a Ward of Court.'

This grabbed Stella's attention.

'A Ward of Court?' It sounded royal. She turned to face him. 'Am I going to live at Buckingham Palace?'

Her hope of becoming Dame Stella Wishbone bubbled to the surface again.

'Not that sort of court.'

Pop went the bubble.

'The local authorities have found a boarding school that will take care of you,' he said, wondering if he had managed to get through. 'I've made the necessary arrangements.'

As before, Stella seemed mesmerised by the swirling snow outside the kitchen window.

'Perfect time to go skiing,' she stated quietly.

'One thing puzzles me. What's happened to your Aunt Zany? I'm surprised she didn't meet you at the airport.'

'She's gone,' Stella replied. 'For good.'

'What do you mean? Where?' He sounded very concerned.

'To Africa. To live in a remote forest. With people she knew when she was a little girl. She was happy there.'

'Your butler said you sent her away but I refused to believe him. Is it true?'

Stella remained silent.

'Oh my goodness. Did you fire her?'

She nodded, unable to speak for sheer shame.

'Stella, aunts are not cannon balls. You can't fire them.'

He frowned, unsure how to proceed.

'Did she leave you a forwarding address?' She nodded.

'You tore it up?' She nodded again.

'I see.'

He took a deep breath and put on a big smile.

'Never mind. I shall track her down forthwith. She's sure to come back when she knows what's happened.'

For all his reassuring words, Mr Beeswax looked extremely worried. He glanced at his watch.

'I have an appointment but it won't take up too much time. While I'm gone, wash and have a spot of breakfast. Then put a few overnight bits and pieces in a bag. Can you do that? I shall return and collect you at midday.'

Her reply did not bode well.

'I'll need my skis.'

'Er... Be ready to leave at twelve o'clock. Do you understand?'

Mr Beeswax reappeared at twelve on the dot. Stella was nowhere to be seen.

She was wandering the streets of London in the falling snow, asking passers-by the way to the nearest ski-slope.

At one point, she boarded a bus.

'Take me to the top of the Matterhorn,' she instructed the driver.

His unhelpful reply was not the one she expected.

'You're fired,' she told him as she got off. 'And you're all fired too,' she shouted at the passengers.

Eventually, she was taken to a police station by a very kind couple who were deeply concerned by her sad behaviour.

Rosa Buvitt and Hugh Jundapance went to a lot of trouble to make sure Stella was placed in safe hands. But, of course, as they said goodbye to her, they were briskly informed that they were fired too.

By the time Mr Beeswax tracked Stella down, she was enjoying a cup of hot chocolate and sandwiches in a warm police station waiting-room, feeling more like her old, sharp self. But even so, and in spite of Mr Beeswax's supportive presence, she took a baleful view of her immediate prospects.

'Then it's all over. I'm ruined. I haven't a sausage.'

'Nonsense. You simply don't have any visible means of support.'

This statement puzzled Stella because she was sitting on a very hard chair. But it was just one of many things that made no sense any more.

'I'm trying to locate your aunt.'

'No, I don't want you to.'

'Why on earth not? I'm sure she'd come back and take care of you.'

Stella shook her head.

'No! I was horrid and ungrateful. I can't ask her to help me.'

'But she's your only relative. I'm sure that – '

'No, I couldn't face her,' Stella insisted firmly. 'She warned me about Stir. I refused to listen. I was quite rude.'

'I'm sorry you feel like that,' he said, but he was secretly glad to catch a glimpse of her old fighting spirit again.

'I suppose my name is in all the newspapers, telling the world what a fool I've been.'

'Not at all. The moment you were robbed, I took out an injunction forthwith, forbidding the press from printing anything about you, or trying to interview you. So you won't be pestered by any journalists.'

'Talking of being robbed,' her voice took on a grim tone, 'how did Stir – Mr Steele get the diamond out of that box?'

'The police think he stole the key from your pocket. Then at some point during the flight, while you were away from your seat, he unlocked the safe and swapped the diamond for the bust of Beethoven. Both the same size.'

'While I was spending a penny! Oh the irony!'

'When you returned, he slipped the key back into your pocket.'

'All those guards. For nothing!'

'Who did you put in charge of the security arrangements?' he asked.

Stella bit her lip and looked down at her cup.

'I see. You made it quite easy for him.'

'He kept telling me I was really clever. Really dim, more like!'

'And the diamond wasn't insured because... ?'

'It was too expensive to insure. Oh, I've been a silly idiot! A stupid fool!'

Stella broke off abruptly, clutching her forehead.

'That's what my mother used to cry out. Silly idiot! Stupid fool! – alone in her lighthouse, as the wind howled and the sea crashed against the rocks.'

'It's called history repeating itself,' Mr Beeswax reflected.

'You can say that again. I'm just a burp in life's big banquet!'

'Well, we must try to make the best of things. Have you heard of a boarding school called PING?'

'Heard of it? I used to own it! The Peckham Institute for the Nervous and Gifted. I sold it six months ago.'

'They have agreed to take you in.'

'Oh no! I can't live there! Oh the irony! The awful irony!' she wailed bitterly.

'Listen, Stella. PING is run by a charming pair called Hugo Furst and his wife, April.'

'My final humiliation. I'm washed up. Ruined!'

'You're not ruined,' he said, smiling. 'You're a bright little girl and you have everything to live for. There's a lot more to life than being too rich for your own good. As I'm sure you'll find out.'

Stella drew a deep, angry breath.

'And please don't tell me I'm fired, Stella, because you don't employ me. Or anyone else now, for that matter.'

Just then, a policewoman joined them. Sergeant Bookham was remarkably tall and, as an admirer put it, 'an arresting beauty who pulled no punches.' She had taken Stella under her wing.

'How was your hot chocolate?' she asked, with a warm Jamaican accent.

'Quite good, I suppose.'

'What else do you say, Stella?' Mr Beeswax prompted.

'I prefer it sprinkled with cinnamon.'

'What else?'

'Oh, I see. Thank you,' she murmured.

'You're welcome, love. We don't do cinnamon here. Just villains.' Bookham gave Stella a friendly wink.

Stella leaned toward her, earnestly.

'Could I ask your professional opinion?'

'Shoot.'

'Do you think the police will catch Stirling Steele?'

'Of course we will. No question.'

She glanced over her shoulder.

'That's the official reply,' she continued, lowering her voice. 'Off the record, hard to say. He's obviously a smart operator.'

'Will I get my diamond back?'

'I personally doubt it. It's way too famous to place on the open market, or even sell to a private collector. No, chances are he's had it cut up by now. Then he'll flog the smaller pieces off separately.'

'I see.'

'That's life. Keep smiling. You win some, you lose some,' she quipped, a bit too casually for Stella's liking.

By the time they left the police station, a heavy fall of snow had turned Mr Beeswax's car into a little igloo.

After clearing the windows, he drove Stella to a clinic where she had to undergo a brief medical test.

A lady psychologist by the name of Dr Courtney Buggs asked Stella several questions to judge whether she was nervous and gifted enough to qualify for PING.

'First, would you describe yourself as nervous?' the doctor asked.

'How would *you* feel if you'd just lost one hundred million pounds and forty-eight pence?'

'Next question, are you gifted?'

'I can say, 'You're fired', in ten languages, including Mandarin. *Nee bay jig-ooh.*'

'Lastly, anything else you can do?'

'I can work out the VAT on a major company's gross yearly turnover, cross my eyes and do the splits at the same time.'

And she was in.

CHAPTER EIGHTEEN

Stella Goes PING

Mr Beeswax was waiting for Stella outside the clinic.

'Mrs Bottom called me on my mobile. Sandy's been moved to a hospice and wants you to pay him a visit. I think it would be a good idea.'

They got inside his car.

'Did you say hospital?'

'No, Stella. He is in a hospice. They are friendly, comfortable places where ill people can go when they need to be taken care of. When... when they might not recover.'

'Oh.'

Sandy was lying in a bed looking very poorly. His mother was sitting next to him, holding his hand.

Stella was shocked at how thin and pale he had become.

'Stella – ' The moment Sandy saw Stella, he struggled to sit up but he was weak and short of breath. 'This is – great.'

'Thank you for coming, Stella,' his mother said. 'Sandy's been looking forward to seeing you so much.'

'Mum says – you've been fantastically busy. Have you had – an exciting time?'

'Well... '

She was about to regale him with her troubles when she caught Mr Beeswax's warning eye.

'Things could be worse,' she lied, unable to imagine how.

'Did you read – the book I gave you?'

'Yes, I did. Well, I started to and... It's terrific.'

She wondered where that book was now. It had vanished along with all her other worldly goods.

'I specially liked the story about the tiny wren,' she said.

'Yes, I did too,' Sandy agreed keenly.

'What story is that, Sandy?' Mr Beeswax asked.

'One of Aesop's fables. You tell it to them, Stella.'

'Yes, please tell us,' Mrs Bottom said. 'I love a good story,'

'All the birds gathered together and decided one of them should be named king, but they couldn't agree who was best. So they held a flying competition. Whoever flew the highest would be proclaimed King of the Birds.

'It looked like the eagle would win easily. But when he'd flown up as high as he could, the wren crept out from under his tail feathers and soared even higher, singing, 'I'm the king, I'm the king!"

'The moral,' Sandy explained, 'is that being clever is better than being powerful.'

'How true,' Mr Beeswax said.

'And that cheating pays,' Stella was tempted to add, but she thought it best to change the subject.

'The wren's got a really peculiar Latin name,' she said.

'Yes. *Troglodytes troglodytes*,' Sandy said, grinning. 'It just means cave dweller.'

Once again, Sandy's enthusiasm delighted Stella.

'I'm sorry I've taken so long to visit you, Sandy. I've been learning to play the cello. What sort of a time have you had lately?'

'I had to stop going out – for walks. I've missed that a lot. But this place is great. I'm enjoying myself. Batty likes it here too. All the visitors come and look at him. Do you want him to sit – on your shoulder?'

The grey parrot was perched on the curtain rail, grooming his red tail feathers.

Without any fears this time, Stella stood on a chair, reached up and allowed Batty to walk onto her hand.

When she turned round, everyone's face was looking up at her. For once, she was the tallest person in the room.

It was as if she were peering at Sandy through the wrong end of a telescope, he seemed so small and far away.

'Could you do me a favour?' Sandy asked.

'How much do you want to borrow?' Stella replied, suspiciously. 'I'm a bit low on cash.'

'It's about Batty. If I don't get better, and I can't look after him any more, would you take care of him for me?'

Stella was so startled by the question, she didn't know how to reply. Her reaction confused her, remembering how much she had wanted the parrot only a few months ago.

'Would you, Stella?' his mother appealed, gazing up at Stella. 'I'm sure it won't be necessary, but it would be lovely if you could.'

Mrs Bottom was smiling, but her eyes had filled with tears.

'Please say yes.'

'Well, I haven't got any bird seed or anything.'

Stella glanced at Mr Beeswax. He gave her a quiet nod.

'But yes, all right. I shall do my best.'

'That's great,' Sandy said. He rested his head back on the pillow, slightly out of breath. 'I'm really glad – about that. Thanks. Batty likes you, Stella.'

As if to prove his point, Batty walked up Stella's arm and perched on her shoulder, to the amusement of everyone.

And in spite of his illness, Sandy was still keen to make Stella laugh.

'Have you heard this one? What does a snowman say – when he starts to melt?'

'I don't know,' she answered. 'What?'

'Snow joke!'

Everyone laughed, but Stella had to pretend. Something about the joke troubled her.

It was dark by the time they arrived at PING.

Stella's first impression was of a very old, grim building. However, the entrance hall echoed with the cheerful chatter of young boys and girls.

'Children!' Stella exclaimed, going rigid with disgust. 'I *hate* children. What are they all doing here?'

'This is a school, Stella,' Mr Beeswax replied, trying to be patient. 'They study here. Some of them are boarders.'

'You don't seriously expect me to *mix* with them. I'm allergic to children. I come out in red patches.'

'Sandy's a child. You get along splendidly with him.'

'I can take them one at a time but not in packets of a hundred!'

'This school has an excellent reputation. You might feel better when you meet the couple who run it.'

'I wouldn't gamble on that if I were you.'

Stella and Mr Beeswax were soon seated facing Hugo and April Furst in their office.

Stella's thoughts were typically uncharitable. 'She looks like a surprised ostrich and he looks like a frog.'

'My husband and I want you to regard PING as your home.'

'I used to regard it as a non tax-deductible, low-yield asset,' Stella commented, to the couple's complete bewilderment.

'She's very good with figures,' Mr Beeswax explained.

Hugo and April were friendly but no-nonsense, hard-working people. Theirs was a difficult job dealing with children with all manner of problems. However, they had never met a child quite like Stella before.

'Did you know that PING was originally PHEW?' Hugo said.

'Excuse me?' Stella queried.

'It first started life,' April explained, 'as the Peckham Home for Excitable Waifs. PHEW!'

'Yes,' her husband went on. 'PHEW was an orphanage, founded by a colourful sea captain called Buster Cutlass-Blister.'

'In 1741,' April added. 'And now it's a school for children who have lost their parents and who are nervous and gifted.'

'And whose talents need special cultivation,' Hugo explained, completing her sentence.

Their way of sharing the conversation reminded Stella of watching a game of ping-pong.

'Many live nearby with foster parents,' said Hugo.

'But some sleep here,' continued April. 'You'll share a room with another little girl called Annie.'

'No, I don't think so,' Stella stated politely but firmly.

Her tone of authority momentarily halted the couple.

'OK. Let's show you where you'll be sleeping tonight,' Hugo suggested, and he led the way out of the office.

'My walk-in wardrobe was twice as big as this bedroom.'

True, it was hardly spacious, but some effort had been made to make it look bright and cheerful. There were two single beds; each had a cupboard for personal belongings.

Colourful pictures decorated the walls and a jug of artificial daisies sat on the window sill.

'Your room-mate Annie is keen on astronomy,' April said, pointing above Stella's head.

A home-made model of the solar system dangled from the ceiling, its multicoloured balls slowly bobbing and revolving, wafted by air currents.

Stella's attention was caught by a boy band poster pinned to the wall beside her bed.

'That's Paul Quickly,' she exclaimed, 'the lead singer with Terrible Breath! He wanted to buy my cello.'

'Paul is one of our most famous ex-pupils,' Hugo said. 'I had no idea he was interested in the cello.'

April was equally surprised.

'All he ever did here was scream loudly and break things.'

Stella couldn't be bothered to explain. And, in any case, a second later she exclaimed, 'Here it is! My cello!'

And there it certainly was, leaning casually in the shadows behind the door, as if to say, 'Nice to see you. Pull up a chair.'

'How did my cello get here?' she asked Mr Beeswax. 'Does it fly about while I'm asleep?'

'I took charge of it the moment you sold your house. I had a feeling you'd want to keep it. This might come in useful, too.'

He handed her the briefcase she used to carry everywhere.

'My bag. No fifty page contracts in it now.'

'Look inside.'

Opening the briefcase, she discovered something she would treasure for the rest of her life.

'Sandy's present,' she whispered softly.

She took out the book and examined it with infinite care.

'You can start your own new library. Forthwith.'

'Do you like my mobile?' a young voice asked.

A plump girl was watching Stella from the doorway.

She moved into the room and dumped her school bag on her bedside table.

'If you blow the planets, they circle round the sun.'

Stella frowned at her. 'I don't blow things.'

'Let me show you.'

The girl raised her face and blew a stream of air towards her mobile. Slowly, the little Earth, Mars, Venus and Jupiter, etc., began to orbit a yellow tennis ball representing the sun.

'My name's Annie Clipps. What's yours?'

Fifteen minutes later, Mr Beeswax was saying his goodbyes.

He looked down at Stella with his serious face.

'I shall call back tomorrow to see how you're getting on. I have something very important to say to you, but it can wait until later. Try to make the best of things here.'

Hugo Furst held the door open.

'Annie will help you to find your sea legs, as they say.'

'Yes,' his wife continued. 'She'll show you the ropes.'

And the three adults left, closing the door.

Stella sank onto her narrow bed, staring gloomily at the floor. The thought of being absorbed into a huge mass of children appalled her.

'I'm like a fly that's fallen splat into a gutter, disappearing down a storm drain,' she thought to herself.

Sometime, somehow, she would find a way to escape...

'I know,' Annie said, sympathetically, perching on the edge of her bed, facing Stella. 'You feel horrible at first, but after a while PING grows on you. It's really good. Do you play that cello?'

'No. I juggle with it.'

Annie wasn't sure if Stella was being funny.

'I'm having two piano lessons a week.'

'Do they teach magic spells? It'll take a powerful one to keep me here.'

Annie laughed hesitantly.

'If you do play the cello, we could have a bash at a duet.'

'I'd rather be left completely alone.' And to underline this, she twisted her shoulders round, presenting her back to Annie.

'Don't you want to be friends?'

Stella growled like an angry terrier.

'I would rather cut off my head and boil it in a pig's bladder. I don't make friends with children. Their company bores me to hacking sobs.'

'Who do you talk to or play with?'

Stella swung her face round and glared angrily at Annie, trying to think of a cutting response. But all this achieved was to make her head spin.

'Would you like a peppermint?' Annie asked timidly, offering her a packet.

'I told you I want to be left alone!'

'Go on. Have a mint. They're good.'

Annie placed a peppermint sweet on the bed beside Stella.

Stella looked at the sweet. She wanted to eat it but she definitely didn't want to appear friendly. What should she do? Her mind was a wobbly blank. She rudely turned her back on Annie again.

A bell sounded.

'Before dinner, our school Governor is giving a speech in the assembly hall. I've been asked to take you with me.'

'I'm staying here.'

'If you change your mind, it's along the corridor and down the stairs. I've got to go because I'm playing the piano.'

Annie waited a moment, in case Stella changed her mind.

Then she left.

Stella closed her eyes. She was feeling very odd, having had little to eat all day. Several children rushed and clomped past the open door. Some peered inside and stared at the newcomer, whispering and giggling. After a few minutes, the noises faded away to silence.

She opened one eye and looked down at the peppermint lying beside her on the bed. It looked as unwanted and out of place as she felt. She popped it into her mouth.

Now it is well known that a strong peppermint on an empty stomach can go straight to a person's head and make them feel woozy.

Stella stood up. The room revolved like Annie's mobile.

'Am I really an excitable waif, or is this all a ghastly dream?'

Curiosity drew her over to the window.

She squinted at the darkness outside. A grey, concrete office block and a grey, concrete wall towered over the snow-covered playground. It couldn't have looked more grim.

'It's like a view from a prison cell,' she thought. 'Where are the stables, the gardens, the tennis courts, the Olympic-sized swimming pool, the acres of woodland?'

A loud cheer came from below.

She staggered out into the corridor and followed the sound to the top of a staircase.

A man's voice could be heard in the distance. Clutching the banister, she descended the stairs to the front lobby.

Tall double doors with glass panels led to the main assembly hall. They were shut.

Stella found a chair, dragged it over to the doors and stood on it to get a clear view of what was going on inside.

It was a sight that turned the blood in her veins to ice.

There were more children than Stella had ever seen together in one place.

In her delirious vision, the tops of thousands and thousands of young heads, like a bobbing ocean, seemed to stretch for ever. In fact, there were only sixty-two.

Stella felt hot and tense with shock.

On a stage at the far end of the hall, the governor, a burly, bearded man wearing a navy-blue blazer, was giving a speech. Behind him, the teachers sat in a row.

'Over the years, PING has suffered many a sea change, but today it still addresses the needs of nervous and gifted children who have no parents. Captain Cutlass-Blister was an orphan himself so he knew all too well about life's treacherous tides and dangerous currents.'

'And boring speeches,' Stella thought.

'That's why he battled against a sea of troubles to found this wonderful school. He was my great, great, great, great grandfather, and I feel proud to stand here and see the fine picture you all make – a splendid flotilla of small craft, all shipshape and Bristol fashion.'

'Aye-aye, captain,' said one of the children.

Everybody laughed, including the governor.

'And so, to celebrate PING's ongoing success, and the man who created this noble old building – '

'This rickety old ruin,' Stella added quietly.

' – let us sing a special song which I know you all love.'

The children gave a loud groan of mock reluctance.

'The Peckham school song!'

Everyone cheered and whistled as Annie Clipps walked onto the stage and sat down at the piano.

She thumped out three stirring chords.

'All together!' the governor shouted, and the whole assembly sang the school song.

> *'Every orphan, big or small,*
> *Tossed upon life's billowing foam,*
> *Shall be welcome, one and all,*
> *Welcome to our Peckham home.'*

'Yes, you certainly are welcome to it,' Stella muttered, scornfully.

> *'Peckham's harbour holds us safe,*
> *Built for orphans of the storm.*
> *Here, for every windblown waif,*
> *Peckham's port is dry and warm!'*

'Peckham's port? Sounds like an old man's drink,' she sneered.

> *'We don't heed the howling gales!*
> *We don't fear the treacherous tide!*
> *Peckham's wind will fill our sails*
> *And swell our hearts with joy and pride!'*

'Peckham's wind? It must be the food they serve.'

'Last verse!' the governor yelled.

> *'Row your boat then, bravely on!*

PING, your loyal Peckham friend,
Will steer you safely till you've gone
Past the rocks and round the bend.'

'Any more of this and I shall go round the bend! I'd rather be wandering the streets.'

'Well done, everyone! Long live PING!'

And a loud cheer went up from all the pupils.

'That's it,' Stella declared. 'I'm out of here.'

She was about to step down from the chair, when a little boy pushed the door open and sent her crashing to the floor.

'Sorry!' he shouted over his shoulder as he dashed off.

In the confusion that followed, Stella was engulfed by a dam burst of children as they poured out of the hall on their way to the school canteen for dinner.

Stella found herself sitting on the floor, rubbing her head. A huge pair of shiny black shoes planted themselves in front of her.

She looked up... Grey trousers with sharp creases... A navy-blue blazer with silver buttons... A bushy beard... The man who had been talking on the stage towered over her, taller and stouter than before, like a skyscraper topped with grey curly hair.

'Ah!' he exclaimed, 'Stella Wishbone, I presume! I've heard fascinating things about you. Why on earth are you sitting on the floor?'

He was joined by Mr and Mrs Furst, who lifted Stella to her feet, extremely concerned for her safety.

'Oh my goodness, are you hurt?' April asked her.

'Look,' Stella gasped, pushing their hands away, 'try to get this straight! There is nothing wrong with me. I'm just not staying here!'

But she was an alarming sight, trembling and swaying from side to side like a palm tree in a tropical storm.

'A little dinghy like you? Alone on the high seas? Where are you heading?' the Bushy Beard asked.

'Tokyo, New York, all points anywhere.'

'But you can barely keep your head above water. What you need, young mariner, is a bowl of hot soup to warm your cockles. Be my guest!'

'No, I'm all right. I'm in good trim and seaworthy. So I'll just turn about and heave ho!' she gibbered, hoping these seafaring terms would satisfy him.

'Come along,' said April Furst, taking Stella by the hand.

'Dinner time,' said Hugo, taking her by the other hand and between them they led Stella gently but firmly to the noisy canteen.

Before long, Stella was indeed seated in front of a bowl of hot soup and crusty bread. However, she felt too queasy to eat anything.

Hugo Furst introduced her to the Bushy Beard.

'This gentleman is the Governor of the school.'

'The name is Commander Keenan Ableforce.' He shook her little hand manfully. 'Very pleased to meet you, Stella.'

His cheerful red nose and cheeks beamed at her like a lighthouse across the canteen table.

'Your story is sadly familiar. One minute you're cruising along in your luxury liner, snug and watertight. The next, you've crashed onto the rocks and you're flung overboard. Mayday! Mayday! Up and down you plunge in the dark waves. Up and down. Up and down.'

'He's making me seasick,' she thought.

'Just as all seems lost – PING, the lifeboat, races to the rescue! You'll be set on dry land in no time.'

Stella's feverish imagination was throbbing with ships and shores. 'I must ask an intelligent question to appear normal,' she thought.

'Are you by any chance a sailor?'

'Clever of you to guess. Thirty years in the British Navy. Runs in the family.'

'You look very hot and bothered, Stella.' April Furst felt her forehead. 'You might be running a slight temperature.'

'You're trembling.' Hugo Furst smelt her breath. 'Are you a peppermint addict?'

Stella stood up, ignoring their concern.

'Could I have your business card, Commander?' she asked.

'Why, er – yes, of course you may.' He was astonished at such a professional manner in one so young. 'Here you are.'

'Interesting talk,' she uttered in a wobbly voice, putting his card in her pocket.

'I'll ring you when my schedule eases up. Meanwhile, that is all for today, ladies and gentlemen. I declare this meeting over.'

She was swaying about even more wildly, as if she were indeed a tempest-tossed boat.

'I shall now hoist something and heave away... Ooh!'

The room suddenly lurched before her and she fell senseless into April Furst's arms.

CHAPTER NINETEEN

Stella Has Mail

The next morning, Stella lay in bed, gazing up at the ceiling.

There were several cracks in it. She made out the shapes of a broken umbrella, a stick insect and a hat.

'What a dump,' she thought.

But even though her new bedroom was shamefully small, she had enjoyed a good night's sleep and was feeling surprisingly well. However, she was determined to be in a grouchy mood.

'This place is falling to bits,' she announced, loudly enough to awake Annie if she wasn't already.

'How are you this morning?' Annie asked, sitting up in bed.

'Terrible. Don't ask. Things couldn't possibly get worse.'

'Why?'

'I've lost everything.'

'What have you lost?'

'I'd rather not talk about it.'

'OK. I was just going to say – '

'In fact,' Stella continued, 'I am never going to speak to anyone ever again. That'll show them.'

'Who?'

'People.'

'Why?'

'Because it will.'

'Show them what?'

'That I'm serious.

'What about?'

'Everything.'

'How?'

Stella ground to a sulky halt. These were tiresome details so she cut straight to the point.

'I have decided to give up in total despair. From now on, I'm not going to look at anyone, or read anything, or eat, or smile, or whistle, or poke out my tongue, or walk anywhere. Not for as long as I live! Till the end of the whole universe!'

'If you never read anything, how will you know what the date is?'

'Won't care.'

'Suppose you have a hospital appointment, how will you know when to go?'

'By asking.'

'You said you're not going to speak to anyone.'

'I shall write down on a piece of paper, 'What is today's date?' and show it to them.'

'Suppose you haven't got a pencil?'

'I'll buy one in a shop.'

'How will you buy one without speaking?'

'I shall go like this.'

Stella threw back her bedclothes and performed an elaborate mime that looked more like a tent flapping in a hurricane.

'But if you're not going to walk anywhere, how will you get to the shop in the first place?'

'On a bicycle.'

This went on for the next hour, during which time they washed and dressed themselves, and Annie took Stella down to the canteen.

Stella demolished a sizeable breakfast for someone determined never to eat again, but she managed to find fault with the Italian napkins in their silver rings. Chiefly because there weren't any.

'Let's see if there's post for you in the letter rack.'

Even though it was her first day at PING, there was indeed a letter waiting for her in the entrance hall.

'Hardly anyone knows I'm here. Who could've... ?'

Stella opened it and read the contents. She looked even more puzzled.

'Hmm... '

'What is it about?' Annie asked, eagerly.

'My Aunt Zany. She used to look after me.'

'Is she all right?'

'I'm not sure. I sent her away because I was angry with her. I wish I hadn't now.'

'Why did you send your aunt away?'

Stella was reluctant to admit how unkindly she had behaved toward her aunt.

'She gave me some boring advice,' she replied evasively, 'and I wouldn't listen to it.'

'Why was it boring?'

'Because it was good, I suppose.'

At that moment, a bell was rung and all the children went to their first class of the morning.

And something strange happened which surprised even Stella.

She attended five classes during the day and, far from giving up in total despair, enjoyed each one. The Biology teacher, Anna Konda, summed up people's opinion of Stella as follows:

'Curious specimen. Flings its weight around, but should settle in nicely when it's acclimatised.'

In Science, Stella quoted the current price of tin.

'Tin doesn't rust. That's why it's valuable. And that's why it was used to make cans. They're aluminium now.'

In Geography, she mentioned that she once flew over the north pole. 'I noticed Iceland was green and Greenland was icy.'

In Biology, she described her pet scorpion, Sarah Nade.

'Sarah only woke up at night and I fed her with moths and mealworms. Unlike people, a scorpion grows its skeleton outside its body, so it's called its exoskeleton. Exo means outside.'

In History, she amused everyone with Sandy's story about Henry VIII's parrot whistling for a ferry to cross the Thames.

And in English, they each took it in turns to read aloud the wonderful Greek myth of King Midas who was given the golden touch and suffered miserably.

'How true,' she reflected aloud. 'A warning to us all.'

It had been a busy day, and come 4.30pm all the pupils were allowed a free hour to amuse themselves.

'Stella, go upstairs and get your cello,' Annie suggested, 'and meet me in the main hall. It's always empty about this time.'

As Stella climbed the stairs to her room, she was surprised to realise that, in spite of being in close contact with children, she had not broken out in red patches. In fact, she had suffered no skin discolouration at all.

A few minutes later, she and Annie were on the stage of the assembly hall, going through a simple duet they both happened to know – Baa Baa Black Sheep.

'Let's play it again, quicker,' Stella urged.

Annie agreed, and they were soon increasing the tempo more and more till they scarcely knew what they were doing, and ended up laughing so helplessly they could barely speak.

'That was very silly,' Annie spluttered.

'Oh let me get my breath back!' Stella gasped. 'You looked really funny. I thought you were going to fall off your stool!'

'If we'd gone any faster, I would've!'

'And my bow would've gone whizzing off like an arrow and hit you on the bottom!'

They both roared with laughter.

Bottom! The word suddenly reminded Stella of her friend, Sandy. She wondered if he was recovering in the hospice.

'Would Stella Wishbone please come to the principal's office.'

Hearing this announcement over the loudspeaker, they both collected their music and books, and agreed to meet later for the evening meal.

'Come in.'

Stella entered the principal's office.

Hugo Furst was seated at his desk.

'Stella, you have a visitor.'

He smiled at Mr Beeswax, who rose from his chair and offered his hand cautiously.

'Hallo Stella,' he said, waiting for her to shout something strange at him.

'Hallo,' she replied, and shook his hand. 'I thought you might be coming.'

'Why?'

'Because you said you would.'

'Oh yes. So I did.'

'We're having tea.' Hugo was about to pour from the pot. 'Would you care for some fruit juice?'

Before Stella could reply, the door leading to the next room opened.

April Furst entered, looking deeply downcast. She closed the door quietly, and then burst into a flood of tears.

'It's no good,' she sobbed. 'He won't budge.'

Hugo gave his wife a comforting hug.

'There, there,' he murmured, patting her softly on the back as if she were a pet dog. 'You did your best. Don't cry.'

Stella gave Mr Beeswax a puzzled look.

'I'm afraid you have arrived at a difficult moment,' he explained to Stella. 'PING has severe problems.'

'Forgive my emotional display,' April gasped, 'but I've been bottling this up for ages. I can't bear that awful man.'

And she dissolved into tears again.

Hugo sat his wife down and poured out a cup of tea for her.

'What's going on? What awful man?' Stella asked.

'PING's new owner has just brought us terrible news about our school,' Hugo confided to her. 'His name is Robin Banks. He is going to tear this building down and replace it with a multi-storey car park.'

'Makes perfect business sense to me,' Stella responded, rather bluntly.

'Oh!' April Furst wailed and blew her nose loudly.

'We were hoping he would sell it to us for a modest sum. But he has refused our final offer.' His voice was husky with emotion. 'PING... will have to close.'

'No it won't,' Stella replied, quietly but very firmly.

'What do you mean?' he asked.

'Never mind. Go on. I'm listening.'

'If we are forced to leave, the school will be homeless because we don't have the money to buy new premises. It will be the end of PING.'

'*For ever!*' April blurted out, making Mr Beeswax drop his teaspoon.

'Look,' Stella said, trying to be patient, 'could you both get a grip and tell me how far you've got with your offer. Not that I care tuppence about this crummy dump. However, I have enjoyed my day here and I've no wish to be shunted off somewhere else.'

'Allow me to clarify.' Mr Beeswax cleared his throat to show he was in command of the situation.

'As you know, Mr Banks owns this building.'

'Yes, I ought to know. I sold it to him.'

'And now, Mr and Mrs Furst are anxious to buy it. They've made him a fair offer, but he is demanding an unreasonably large sum of money.'

'Money which we don't have,' April managed to gulp out.

'But we've been trying to raise,' her husband added. 'He's in the next room.'

'With all the papers,' April lamented. 'Smoking his horrible cigar.'

'In there?' Stella asked, pointing to the door.

'Yes.'

'He is.'

'Well I never! Leave it to me. I'll have a private word.'

April was drying her eyes on a tea towel.

'What do you mean?'

'Banksie and I have done business together. We go back a long way.'

'But Stella,' April began, 'you are far too young to understand. Mr Banks is a – '

'Do you want to keep this building or don't you?'

'Of course,' Hugo insisted.

'OK then.' She gave a crafty smile. 'Let me change his mind for him.'

'It's worth a try,' Mr Beeswax offered.

Mr and Mrs Furst remained doubtful.

'This is highly irregular, to say the least,' Hugo said.

'Trust me,' Stella said.

April's ostrich eyes widened. 'Yes, but... '

'Trust me,' Stella repeated firmly.

Hugo's frown deepened. 'That's all very well but... '

'Trust me,' she sighed, with a heavenward glance.

'I have seen Stella in action,' Mr Beeswax reassured them,

'and believe me, this young lady can be – and I choose the phrase carefully – very persuasive.'

'But Stella, what could you possibly say?' asked Hugo, mystified.

'Well... how shall I put it?' Stella leaned forward and lowered her voice.

'I know where the bodies are buried.'

For several seconds, April and Hugo Furst stared at her in speechless disbelief.

'Just give me fifteen minutes with him.'

Hugo and April turned to Mr Beeswax.

'She might surprise you.'

'What have we to lose?' Hugo asked his wife.

April bit her lower lip. 'So be it,' she murmured.

Blinking nervously, they both faced Stella and nodded their assent.

'Good.' Stella marched over to the door and gave three smart knocks.

'Come in!' growled a gruff voice.

Stella opened the door and entered the room.

'How's tricks, Banksie?'

The adults heard a sharp intake of breath.

'You! What in the name of two-timing takeovers are you doing here?'

'Oh, I just happened to be in the area, and I thought the two of us should have a little chat. About your plans for this building.'

And she closed the door. Firmly.

There was an uncomfortable pause as the adults tried to imagine what was going on in the adjoining room.

April Furst clutched her husband's arm, anxiously.

'Do you think that was just a turn of phrase about the buried bodies?'

'I haven't a clue.' He turned to Mr Beeswax. 'Did she mean... real bodies?'

Mr Beeswax became completely confused and whipped off his spectacles, trying to look intelligent.

'Oh, I'm sure not!' He forced a laugh. 'No, it was merely a figure of speech. You see... '

He gestured broadly with his glasses. They flew across the room and landed in the paper-bin.

'You see, business people,' he continued, delving into the bin, 'get up to all manner of... '

'Mischief?' April suggested.

'By no means! No, not at all! I mean they employ all kinds of methods to... '

'To silence people?' Hugo prompted.

'No no. To get rid of difficult... I mean, to settle a problem.'

He fished his glasses out of the bin, put them on again and gave a nervous cough.

'Look, I suggest we all relax while we're waiting. Let's pour ourselves another cup of tea and talk about something pleasant. Aren't puppies nice?'

So for the next quarter of an hour, they drank tea and talked about puppies.

Then a long silence fell.

April glanced over at the closed door.

'She is the most unnerving child I have ever met,' she quietly admitted. 'And I have met a few.'

At that moment, quite unexpectedly, the door burst open.

There, to everyone's astonishment, stood a fat and furious Robin Banks, his face like a painful blister. He slammed the door behind him.

'The building is yours!' he barked, flinging a piece of paper onto the desk.

'That's the signed agreement. And this is a written statement I shall be sending to the newspapers. It reads, I quote: *As a keen fundraiser for many charities, I am donating this building to you, the directors of PING, free of charge,*' he snarled. '*You will be able to continue your wonderful work, helping nervous and gifted children to reach their full potential,*' his eyes narrowed meanly, '*such as my young business colleague, Stella Wishbone, who has fallen on hard times.* Unquote.'

'Oh, Mr Banks! This is magnificent!' April trilled like a nightingale.

'Where is Stella?' her husband asked. 'We must thank her.'

'Thank *her?!*'

Mr Banks turned his cold stare onto them as if he were about to spray them with machine gun bullets.

'*Thank her?!* I shall expect paragraphs of abject thanks from you to *me personally* in all the national papers.'

He stubbed out his cigar in the sugar bowl.

'I have no more to add,' he snapped, rigid with rage, and barged out of the office.

April Furst picked up the signed agreement as if it had been dropped there by a chorus of angels.

'It is a miracle. Look, Hugo!'

Hugo was amazed. 'But how did she – ? What did she – ?'

Mr Beeswax put on his cool command voice.

'May I see?' They awaited his expert legal opinion.

After a swift perusal he handed the agreement back to April.

'Everything seems to be in order. I shall sort out the details forthwith. The school is yours.'

The door to the next room opened.

'Sorted!' Stella said, as she rejoined them in the office.

'I had to make a phone call. Has Banksie gone already?'

She was greeted with a fountain of praise and gratitude from the Fursts, but above all there was one urgent question.

'What did you say to him?'

'I think I'd better keep that information under wraps,' she said gravely. 'For your own safety.'

In the stunned silence, April gave a loud nervous gulp.

'How is the fruit juice situation?' Stella asked.

'One orange juice coming up,' Hugo cried, rushing to the fridge, 'and a fresh pot of tea for three to celebrate!'

He busily poured out a drink for Stella as April put the kettle on and washed out the cups in a haze of happiness.

'What are you smiling about, Stella?' Mr Beeswax asked.

'Banksie. He's going to feel a bit sore for a couple of days, but he'll get over it. You were lucky. That mean old crook has been fishing for a knighthood for the past year. This will clinch it.'

'How can we ever thank you, Stella?' April asked.

'Some ice cream would be nice.'

'Of course!' her husband cried.

'I'd like three scoops. Banana, chocolate and lemon.'

Mr Beeswax cleared his throat and gave Stella a meaningful look.

'Please,' she added.

'I'm afraid we only have vanilla,' Hugo said.

'But we could add some tinned pineapple chunks,' his wife suggested, drying the teacups.

'It's a deal,' Stella responded, and she slapped the desk.

'Who were you ringing?' Mr Beeswax inquired.

'Someone called Paul Quickly – a famous pop star. He was once a pupil here, according to Mr Furst.'

'It's true,' Hugo said, handing Stella a glass of orange juice. 'How did you meet him?'

'Paul and I were recently involved in a business deal that didn't work out. I never forget a phone number.'

Mr Beeswax was puzzled.

'But why did you phone him just now?'

'I told him what a shocking state this place is in, so he has agreed to do a fundraising concert with his group. All the profits will go to PING.'

'Oh!' April exclaimed, trembling with excitement.

The cups and saucers clattered so noisily on her tray, she had to put it down.

'There's nothing wrong with this building that a complete makeover wouldn't cure,' Stella went on. 'With the sale of the TV rights and the live recording, plus a matching contribution from the government, you should clear about two to three million.'

The adults gazed at her in open-mouthed astonishment.

'Anything else you want me to sort out?'

CHAPTER TWENTY

Something for Nothing

'There are two things I came here to tell you.'

Mr Beeswax sat facing Stella in her little room. She was planted cross-legged on her bed and he had balanced himself awkwardly on a stool.

Between them, on the floor, was a large object covered in a red cloth.

'The first is – '

'About my Aunt Zany?' she asked, finishing her ice cream.

Her question clearly made him uncomfortable.

'No no! Nothing to do with your aunt. Nothing remotely,' he insisted, trying to look casual by leaning on a bedside table. His elbow slipped and he almost fell off the stool.

'How is Miss Handlebar?' he asked, recovering his composure.

'I don't know, but this came for me in today's post.'

Stella held up the letter she had received.

'What's that?' he asked innocently.

'It's about my Aunt Zany. It says –

Dear Miss Wishbone, I am an anonymous well-wisher and I am writing to tell you that certain mysteries involving your cello will be solved, forthwith, if you contact your aunt at the following address: PO Box 4, Marimba Road, Tanzania, Africa.'

Mr Beeswax narrowed his eyes, as if thoroughly puzzled.

'Hmm... ' he said.

'That's exactly what I said. Hmm... '

'I wonder who wrote it,' he mused.

'You did.'

'No I didn't. It wasn't me. How did you guess?'

'Because you signed it.'

'Oh.'

'You put *Yours faithfully, Basil Beeswax* at the bottom.'

'I sign everything in the out-tray before going home. Force of habit.'

'And you used your solicitors' stationery with the address printed on the top. That was another important clue.'

He shook his head. 'It's always a tiny detail that gives one away.'

'Never mind. It was nice to get a letter.'

'Perhaps I was hoping, deep down, that you would realise I'd sent it,' he said, unable to look her in the eye.

'Why didn't you just tell me where Aunt Zany went?'

'Because I'm not supposed to be involved any more.'

'I don't understand.'

'It's what she wanted. Allow me to explain. The last time I spoke to your aunt, I told her I had fallen hopelessly in love with her and I begged her to marry me, forthwith.'

Stella stared at him, unable to imagine how this neat man, who always behaved correctly, apart from the occasional droppage, could harbour such unruly feelings toward her aunt.

'But to my disappointment she made a lot of rattling noises and said, '*No, it is impossible. You must go away.*' Then she burst into bitter tears and cried out, '*Our paths must never cross again! Never, never, never!*' She made it very clear.'

'How?'

'Because she burst into bitter tears and cried out, '*Our paths must never cross again! Never, never, never!*'' he repeated, slightly impatiently.

'Oh yes, I see. I'm sorry. I still feel a bit woozy from yesterday's peppermint. Didn't she give you a reason?'

'I begged her to but she wouldn't.'

'So how did you track down her address? I tore it up into lots of pieces.'

'They were in your filing cabinet, stored under T for *Torn Up Addresses*. I glued them together again.'

'Oh yes! Force of habit, like you,' Stella said, smiling ruefully. 'My father taught me to do that. He often used to say, '*Never throw away addresses or death threats. It's surprising how often they come in useful.*' He was right!'

Now it was Mr Beeswax's turn to stare.

But her smile quickly faded.

'I'm puzzled. What did you mean in your letter about mysteries involving Aunt Zany and my cello?'

'There's something strange about your aunt.'

'The rattling? You get used to it.'

'No, it's something else. I can't put my finger on it, but I strongly suspect she is harbouring a secret. A dark and terrible secret. To do with that cello.'

They both looked at the instrument.

As usual, it was leaning in the corner behind the door. It seemed to be enjoying a comfy nap.

'It's odd you should say that,' Stella observed. 'I began to wonder if it was alive. First, it vanished and reappeared like magic. Then I dreamt it could fly and talk. And then it played music to me at night. It's true! I heard it clearly when I was half asleep. I even remember one of the tunes.'

'If you contact your aunt, she might be able to clear up the mystery. I'm sure she'd be delighted to hear from you. She might even invite you to go and live with her.'

'Do you still love Aunt Zany?' she asked sadly.

He sat bolt upright, looking deeply ill at ease.

'It's a thing of the past. I must try to forget her.'

'I'm the one to blame. If I hadn't been such a terrible handful, she might have agreed to marry you. I'm sorry, Mr Beeswax.'

'Be that as it may,' he answered, trying to force a smile. 'I was about to – '

An ear-shattering whistle made them both jump. It came from the curious object he had placed on the floor between them.

'I think you can guess who this is.'

He removed the red cloth, revealing a bird cage.

'It's Batty! What a lovely surprise.'

The parrot leaned from side to side on his perch, then he scratched his ear vigorously.

'He's yours now Stella. If you're still willing to have him.'

'But he belongs to Sandy.'

'Not any more,' he replied, quietly.

'Won't he miss him if I – ?'

She broke off, realising what this might mean.

'Is Sandy all right?'

'No, Stella. I have very sad news for you about your young friend. Sandy died last night. I'm very sorry.'

There was a silence between them as Stella struggled to understand what he had said.

'But I don't want him to die. Can't they help him?'

She faltered, looking helpless.

'So does that mean –I won't see Sandy again?'

'No, I'm afraid not. I know how sad it is to lose someone you are fond of. But I decided it was important that you should be told.'

Stella looked up at Annie's model of the solar system hanging above their heads.

'Do you think dying is like going to the moon?'

Mr Beeswax blinked at her.

'It wouldn't surprise me at all.'

'That's what Sandy thought. He wasn't afraid. He said it would be interesting. He was most unusual. He knew more about birds than anyone I've ever met.'

She opened her briefcase and took out the book Sandy had given her.

'Look at this picture.'

She showed Mr Beeswax a beautiful illustration of a goldfinch with bright yellow, red and black feathers.

'They perch on thistles and pick out the seeds without getting scratched.'

'Very clever.'

'They are! And a whole flock of them is called a charm of goldfinches.'

She closed the book.

'I only met Sandy twice altogether but he was very friendly. I really, really liked him. He made me laugh.'

She touched the cover of the book gently, as if to make sure it was really there.

'I'm never going to forget him. Not ever.'

'Of course you won't.'

Stella's tears took her by surprise. Mr Beeswax gave her a clean handkerchief and comforted her.

'*I just can't cope!*' Batty exclaimed in Aunt Zany's voice.

'Sandy liked you too, Stella,' Mr Beeswax said. 'That's why he specially asked for you to look after his parrot.'

'I won't be able to,' Stella said, wiping her nose.

'Why?'

'Because I've given up in total despair.'

'Dear me. That seems a pity.'

The parrot looked at Stella with a beady eye, his head on one side, and said, '*Move along inside, please.*'

'Correct me if I'm wrong, Stella, but you sounded more optimistic today.'

'It's just a mask. Deep down, I see how badly I've behaved.'

'I think you're being a bit hard on yourself.'

'No. It's all my fault. I take full blame.'

'Look. I've checked with the teachers. They say Batty can live in the staff room.'

Batty gave a stretch and flapped his wings.

'He wants to be let out,' Stella said.

She opened the cage and offered her hand to Batty.

He thought it over for a moment, edged to the cage door and then stepped out carefully onto her finger.

Mr Beeswax leaned back a little warily.

Stella sighed, studying Batty's beautiful feathers.

'*Things can't possibly get worse,*' she muttered grimly.

She placed Batty on top of the cage, where he looked all around the room, as if sizing it up.

'Well, if things can't get worse,' Mr Beeswax replied quite logically, 'it means they can only get better.'

'That's true enough.'

'Here's an idea. Draw a picture of Batty and we'll send it to Sandy's mother, as a way of saying thank you. It would be a kind thing to do. She's feeling very sad.'

Stella frowned. 'But I don't know how to draw. I've never drawn anything – except pie charts and profit lines going up or down.'

'I'm sure Mrs Bottom will be delighted with whatever you send her. Maybe one of your teachers could help you to... '

He faltered, catching sight of Stella's face.

She was leaning forward and gazing closely at Batty with an expression Mr Beeswax had never seen before.

'All right, then. I will,' she said softly. 'I'll draw the best picture of Batty in the whole world!' Her eyes shone with a brilliance that seemed to brighten the room.

'I never want to be rich again. I could've easily squeezed a load of cash out of Banksie just now. But what would I do with it? Buy another stupid diamond?'

Her words were fierce and yet carefully chosen.

'Honestly, if Sergeant Bookham walked through the door right now and gave me back the Cripes Diamond, I'd throw it out of the window! It *is* cursed. It's brought me nothing but bad luck.'

'That may or may not be the case, Stella. The strange fact is that money is neither good nor bad. It's what people *do* with it that helps or harms them. As for luck – some say we *make* our own luck, whether good or bad.'

'Batty's name comes from the Swahili word for good luck.'

'How interesting.'

Stella placed her finger in front of Batty's feet. He slowly stepped onto it as if he'd been waiting for a bus.

'Well, you never know,' Mr Beeswax continued. 'Batty might bring you good luck one day, in a way that you can't even begin to imagine!'

'How?'

'In a way that you can't even begin to imagine,' he repeated.

'Oh yes, I understand,' she said. 'Sorry. I'm still a bit out of sorts.'

'It's hardly surprising. A lot has happened to you in the last few days. I think it would be a great shame if you gave up in total despair.'

'You're right. I won't. I've changed my mind.'

There was an odd chirping noise.

'That's not coming from Batty,' Stella said.

'It's me,' Mr Beeswax admitted, looking slightly flustered and feeling his pockets. 'Excuse me for one moment, Stella.'

In spite of her earlier resolution, Stella smiled broadly.

For the first time, she realised that Mr Beeswax was, in fact, a very likeable person, so different from her initial impression.

Mr Beeswax eventually found his mobile phone and took the call.

'Hello? Speaking... Ah yes! I did get your message. Thank you.'

After listening for a few seconds, he looked at Stella.

'I'm with her now. Would you like to – ? No, not yet... Yes, of course. Here she is.'

Mr Beeswax seemed very pleased about something.

'This is the second thing I had to tell you. About your cello. It's Miss Backenforth. She'd like a word.'

He handed the phone to Stella.

'Hello?'

'Is that Stella?'

'Yes.'

'Good. This is Wanda Backenforth. How are you? I hear you've been off your feed.'

'Mr Beeswax said it's because a lot has happened to me in the last few days. I've been given a parrot.'

'Good gracious! What is his name?'

'Batty. He's walking up my arm. Now he's standing on my shoulder! It feels funny.'

'What a wonderful picture.'

'*Silly idiot!*'

'I beg your pardon.'

'That wasn't me! Batty said it.'

'That's a relief. The reason I'm ringing you, Stella, is to tell you I live very near PING and I'd be quite happy for you to come here for a cello lesson once a week, if you're still interested. How about it?'

'I can't.'

'Why not?'

'Because I'm broke. I don't possess a single, solitary bean.'

'I'm aware of that. The money doesn't matter. The important thing is that you carry on learning the cello.'

'Money *does* matter,' Stella corrected her solemnly, 'when you don't have any. You can't teach me for nothing.'

'Isn't that for me to decide? Listen, Stella. You are a very responsive pupil. I told you. You have a feeling for the cello. It would be a great shame if you chucked it in at this point. And I wouldn't be teaching you for nothing. I would enjoy watching you improve and develop. Sometimes that means a great deal more to a teacher than money.'

'More than money!?' exclaimed Stella in disbelief.

'I said sometimes.'

Stella noticed Mr Beeswax's enquiring gaze.

'Miss Backenforth has offered to give me cello lessons for nothing.'

'What do you say?'

'Thank you, Miss Backenforth. Ooh!'

Batty had chosen that moment to nibble Stella's ear very gently.

'What are you laughing at, Stella?'

'It's Batty. He's tickling my ear. Stop it.'

'It sounds as if you are having fun at PING. Before I go, may I ask you a question?'

'Yes.'

'Have you heard the phrase, there are some things in life that money can't buy?'

'Yes, but I didn't understand what it meant until a friend of mine was very ill, and even money couldn't pay to make him better and he died last night and he was my special friend.'

'Oh dear. I'm very sorry. You see, it's true. Money isn't everything. Obviously, I can't afford to teach all my pupils for nothing, but let's just say teaching you is a way of repaying an old debt.

'A long time ago, when I was born, my parents were very poor. They lived in a house with no bathroom and a toilet in the backyard. My father pulled a drawer out of the sideboard, and that was my cradle! When I grew older, not much older than you, I was given my first cello lesson by a lady who, I later discovered, agreed to teach me for no fee. She expected me to practise, as I hope you will, but she never asked for a penny. Maybe you'll do the same for someone else one day.'

For the very first time in her life, Stella was speechless. The idea that she – the daughter of Ivor Wishbone, one of the meanest millionaires on earth – should give something to someone, *for nothing in return*, was completely new to her. It was like opening a door and beholding a vast, unfamiliar landscape.

'I also believe that the secret of happiness lies in sharing. We take from this world and we must give back. You are too young yet to understand this, but it's an idea for you to think about. Things get badly out of balance if we take, take, take all the time.'

They were words that Stella would remember for the rest of her life.

'*Things can't possibly get worse.*'

'Oh Stella, I know this isn't an easy time for you but please don't say that.'

'I didn't say it,' Stella answered giggling. 'It was Batty!'

The parrot shook himself all over, like a twirled feather duster, and gave another ear-piercing whistle.

For several minutes, none of them could speak for laughing.

Over the next three months, Stella settled down in her new home and grew to enjoy a completely different way of life.

Annie Clipps even showed her how to make her own bed – a thing Stella had never done before.

She worked hard at her lessons, ate well and, after each busy day, slept soundly. The result was that she began to look and feel healthier, and didn't lose her temper so easily.

She read Sandy's bird book again from cover to cover, remembering the day she spent with her 'unusual' friend.

'He wanted to work in a bird sanctuary,' she recalled. 'One day, I shall create a whole wildlife reserve and name it after Sandy. I don't know how, but I will!'

Coming from Stella, as we have seen, such statements were not idle boasts. When she made up her mind to do something, she meant business.

Batty turned out to be a very popular visitor in all the classrooms. He even attended the morning assembly and was adopted as the school mascot.

But one morning, he was perched on Stella's shoulder in the playground when a low-flying plane passed noisily overhead. Batty looked up, squawked, spread his wings wide and flew away after it.

Stella waited for as long as she could, but he didn't return.

'Maybe he'll come back tomorrow,' Annie suggested.

'No. I think he's flown to Africa to be with Aunt Zany. That's where he was born.'

Batty's quirky presence was greatly missed at PING, and so were his startling comments.

However, Stella had an odd feeling that her feathered chum would somehow turn up again, so she wasn't as sad as she expected to be.

CHAPTER TWENTY-ONE

Thunder and Lightning

It would be ridiculous to imagine that a tough operator like Stella would settle for a bowl of ice cream in exchange for saving a whole school from being bulldozed to the ground.

One afternoon, she knocked on the principal's door.

'I've given this a lot of thought. I want two things. One will cost you nothing, and the other will cost you less than fifty pence.'

Mr and Mrs Furst braced themselves. What was coming?

'Yes?'

'I want a day off school.'

'And?'

'I need to make a telephone call. To Portsmouth.'

Stella rang the number and waited.

'Hallo?' a man answered in a brisk, nautical fashion.

'Is that Commander Keenan Ableforce?'

'Speaking. How may I help you?'

'This is Stella Wishbone.'

'Ah, the young lady who asked me for my card. How are you?'

'Do you know anything about lighthouses?'

'I certainly do.'

'I'm trying to find one.'

'They come in all shapes and sizes. Any one in particular?'

'Yes. The one my mother used to live in.'

'That's not much to go on. Do you know its name?'

'No.'

'How about the nearest port?'

'Not the foggiest. But on dark, stormy nights, passing ships used to hear her playing heart-rending music on the cello.'

'That one!'

'Do you know where it is?'

'By an odd coincidence, my ship nearly crashed into it five years ago.'

'I want to go there.'

'This can be arranged.'

Mr Beeswax was baffled.

'But Stella, why do you want to go there?'

'To see the place where my mother lived. I've been given a whole day off school, but I'm not allowed to travel alone.'

'I should think not!'

'So I want you to accompany me as a responsible adult. The Commander is sending a helicopter to fly us to his ship in Portsmouth. He'll show us the engine-room and then we sail to Small Island.'

'Well... '

'Look, I used to be the richest little girl in the world. Now, my only personal possessions are a yellow cello and a book about birds. I don't even have a photograph of my mother. Every single one of them was torn up by my father. And just to show how annoyed he was, he didn't file the pieces!'

Mr Beeswax became flustered.

'Of course I understand your feelings. My only concern is it might be – disappointing for you. It's just an empty lighthouse, locked up and deserted. You won't even be able to go inside.'

'But my mother lived there and I want to see it for myself. OK? We go on Sunday.'

'Very well. But once we've seen it, we turn right round and catch the next boat back. Forthwith.'

'Deal. I mean, thank you. What does 'forthwith' mean?'

'At once.'

They were piped aboard HMS Sea Cucumber and then drank orange juice with the Commander, making maritime small talk.

'Nice to meet up with you again, Stella,' he beamed.

'Why did your ship nearly crash into my mother's lighthouse?'

'She let the lantern go out,' he explained.

'That's because she was sad.'

'I see.'

Ten minutes later, it was full steam ahead.

To amuse his guests, the Commander proudly showed Stella and Mr Beeswax the engine-room.

Two hours later, he took them up to the bridge and pointed to a speck on the horizon.

'That's Small Island. It was named Small Island because it's not very large. And over there is your lighthouse. Blinking Rock it's called. My crew have a ruder name for it.'

'What name?' she asked.

He thought for two seconds.

'Very Annoying Rock. Here, take a look.'

He handed her a heavy pair of binoculars.

'You can see the lighthouse – to the left of the island.'

Stella looked through the binoculars and there it was! Blinking Rock Lighthouse.

'Who switches on the flashing light?'

'No one. They work automatically these days.'

'Mr Beeswax says people don't live there any more.'

'I believe he's right. It was put up for sale some while ago, but it's remained empty. Not surprised. A rather lonely place to live.'

'How can I get to the front door?'

'There is a cobblestone pathway that leads from the island over to Blinking Rock. It's under the sea most of the time. You can only walk across to the lighthouse at low tide.'

The Commander paused, his blue eyes sharper than ever.

'A word of warning, though. That path is very dangerous.'

Mr Beeswax looked highly alarmed.

'I wouldn't advise a visit today,' the Commander continued. 'The forecast is a bit nasty. However, if you insist on taking a closer look – '

'I do,' Stella stated firmly.

'Spoken like a brave sailor. In which case, you had better borrow this.'

He handed Mr Beeswax a large umbrella.

'Good luck!' shouted the Commander.

All the sailors cheered as Stella and Mr Beeswax climbed over the side of the ship and down a ladder into a rowing boat. They were then ferried over to Small Island.

Safely on the harbour steps, they waved goodbye to the rowing crew, and then proceeded to follow a rough track that bordered the island's twisty shore.

Turning a corner, Stella halted abruptly, gazing straight ahead.

'There it is!' she exclaimed, in an excited whisper. 'My mother's lighthouse!'

Before them stood the tall, lonely tower, its flashing light warning passing navigators of the jagged rocks just below the sea. When it was switched on.

They hurried down to the pebbly beach.

It was low tide, conveniently, and, just as the Commander had described, a raised footpath led across the sea to the lighthouse. Stella and her responsible adult began to walk carefully over its slippery cobblestones.

The sky was growing dark.

A strong breeze began to blow. When they were halfway along the path, the breeze turned into a fierce wind and big drops of rain landed on them.

'Dear me, Stella. I'm afraid a storm is building up.'

Lightning flashed. Thunder banged and rumbled all around. Huge waves pounded the narrow walkway on either side, like hands reaching up, trying to drag both of them into the deep.

'Isn't it exciting?!' she answered, her eyes sparkling.

Heavy rain was soon pelting down. Mr Beeswax opened the umbrella, but almost immediately an unexpected gust of wind wrenched it out of his hand, and away it flew, high up into the stormy sky, tumbling and twisting.

'Come along, Stella! Nearly there! Hold on to my arm!'

He had to yell to be heard over the wild weather.

Clinging tightly to one another, they ran slipping and stumbling along the uneven path and then up the steps to the front door of the lighthouse.

Stella was out of breath but laughing.

'I thought we were going to be blown into the sea!'

Mr Beeswax wiped the rain from his serious face.

'You've seen the lighthouse. I suggest that we shelter here in the doorway for a few moments, and then make a dash for it before the tide rises.'

But Stella had other ideas.

'I'm going to ring the doorbell.'

'What for? Nobody lives here.'

He pointed to a FOR SALE sign swinging wildly back and forth in the wind.

'It's deserted.'

'I still want to ring.' She stood on tiptoe but the doorbell remained out of her reach.

'I'll do it,' Mr Beeswax offered.

'No, *I* want to ring it!' Stella insisted. 'Lift me up!'

Mr Beeswax gave her one of his meaningful looks.

'Please!'

He obliged.

Stella pressed the brass doorbell. No answer.

'It doesn't seem to be working,' he said.

'Let me try the knocker.'

Bang bang bang! No answer.

'Come along, Stella. We're soaking wet. Let's get back to the island before the tide cuts us off.'

'But there's a light on upstairs!'

'Of course there is. It's a lighthouse,' he pointed out. 'That's what they do.'

'No, I mean in the top window! Someone's at home. Look! The curtains are drawn and there's a light on.'

She turned to face him with a dramatic gasp. 'Listen!'

'Listen to what?'

'Sh!' she insisted. 'Can't you hear it?'

They waited.

Was it the howling of the tempest? Or was there a strange sound coming from above – from the top of the tower? It was hard to believe, but it sounded exactly like a sad piece of music being played on a cello.

Mr Beeswax was astonished. 'It's – it's not possible,' he stammered. 'It must be an optical illusion! I mean ... the sort you can hear.'

'I'm going in,' Stella declared.

'No, you musn't,' he objected. 'That's trespassing.'

But Stella tried the door. It opened and in she went.

Mr Beeswax smartly scuttled in after her and closed the door behind him.

Complete darkness.

'Where are you, Mr Beeswax? I can't see you.'

'I'm over here.'

But where was here?

Gradually, the shadows formed themselves into dim shapes.

'I think I've found a staircase,' Stella said.

Mr Beeswax joined her at the bottom step.

And now, away from the hubbub of the tempest, the sound of the cello could be heard quite unmistakably. Its voice seemed to be woven out of the very darkness itself.

'I must apologise forthwith, Stella. You were right. Someone is playing a cello.'

'Or some-*thing*.'

Her words gave Mr Beeswax quite a turn, but he pretended to be completely calm about the situation.

'I'm sure there's an entirely rational explanation,' he said.

'On dark, stormy nights, my mother used to play the cello,' Stella whispered in amazement.

For a while they both stood spellbound, as the passionately soulful music resonated down the stairwell, accompanied by a moaning wind.

'Do you think it's her ghost?'

'Of course not,' he replied, trying to force a laugh.

'I'm going to find out.'

Stella placed her foot on the first step.

'One,' she said.

At that moment, flashes of lightning zigzagged through a porthole window, as if to guide her way. Or to warn her.

Thunder growled as she started to climb the spiral stairs. Mr Beeswax followed, keeping a few paces behind her. And all the while, the cello's mournful melody grew louder and louder.

Stella continued to count.

'Twenty-eight. Twenty-nine.'

Grumble, grumble went the thunder.

'Somewhere on this creepy staircase,' Stella thought, 'my mother died.'

Up and up and round and round she proceeded, as torrential rain and sea spray lashed the windows.

'Forty-one. Forty-two.'

The music was growing clearer by the moment.

'That's a very sad tune,' she thought to herself, 'but I like it. It's good.'

Lightning flashes danced crazily about the walls.

'Fifty-nine. Sixty.'

She faltered as a thought struck her.

'How odd. That piece of music... I've a funny feeling I've heard it before. It reminds me of something. But what?'

Thunder bellowed and groaned, like a monster in torment.

'Seventy-seven. Seventy-eight.'

She continued to climb, struggling to work out why the haunting melody sounded so familiar.

'Not a TV advertisement... Ninety-four... Not a film... Ninety-five... '

The next moment, the answer came to her.

She couldn't have been more surprised if she'd been slapped on the arm by a ten stone haddock.

'Of course!' she gasped, coming to a stop, slightly out of breath.

'Mr Beeswax,' she whispered urgently, 'I remember exactly where I've heard that tune before.' She could hardly form the words.

'In my dreams!'

But Mr Beeswax did not reply.

'It's true!' she continued. 'It's the same melody I used to hear playing when I was half asleep.'

She turned around to face him. Nobody.

'Mr Beeswax?'

No answer.

The steps curved away into the gloomy shadows beneath.

'Perhaps he paused for a rest,' she thought. 'I'll wait for him to catch up with me.' But there was no sign of him.

'Where are you, Mr Beeswax!?'

Still no answer.

Only the howling of the wind as it mingled with the cello's yearning notes. Mr Beeswax had vanished.

'Everything is so strange,' she thought, 'like one of my dreams.'

She knew the wisest course would be to retrace her steps and find Mr Beeswax.

'No. I've come this far – so I shall keep going. Even if it means facing a ghost, alone.'

And, as if in a dream, she resumed climbing.

'A hundred and ten. A hundred and eleven.'

Whatever unearthly, music-loving presence was waiting for her above, her sense of purpose was far stronger than her fears.

A few seconds later, the top step appeared.

'A hundred and twenty-one. One hundred and twenty-two.'

She could see a door. It was slightly ajar.

'Hallo?' she said in a nervous whisper. 'Can I come in?'

She knocked and pushed at the door gently. It opened and she entered.

To her complete surprise, she found herself standing in a warm, cosy sitting-room.

And Stella was looking at two very familiar faces.

CHAPTER TWENTY-TWO

Surprise Surprise

'*Silly idiot,*' said Batty from the top of a bookshelf, standing on one leg and stretching the other behind him like a ballet dancer.

That was one familiar face. And the other?

'Stupid fool,' Aunt Zany muttered in reply.

She was gazing into a flickering coal fire from the comfort of an armchair.

'Aunt Zany,' whispered Stella, barely able to speak. 'You're supposed to be in Africa!' Which is exactly where her aunt was at that particular moment – thousands of miles away, lost in her thoughts, remembering happier times.

Her aunt turned and stared at her unexpected visitor with an open mouth.

'Stella!'

She sprang out of her chair like a startled springbok.

'Where did you – ? How did you – ? I can't believe my eyes! What on earth are you doing here?'

'I rang the bell and knocked on the door but no one answered, so I let myself in. Where's that music coming from?'

'One moment.'

Her aunt went to an old-fashioned gramophone and switched it off.

'A record! I thought a ghost was playing.'

'This is the most wonderful surprise, Stella! But I don't understand. How did you get here? Who is with you? Surely you didn't come all this way by yourself.'

'No. I didn't. I'm with – '

She looked over at the door, but her responsible adult still hadn't appeared. She ran to the stairwell and called.

'Mr Beeswax!'

Still no answer.

'You shouldn't be here, Stella.'

'Why?'

Her aunt seemed strangely agitated.

'Mr Beeswax must take you home immediately.'

Stella was tempted to stamp her foot and shout, but she realised that was her old way of dealing with problems, and look where it had landed her.

'I'm really sorry I sent you away, Aunt Zany.'

'No. It was my own fault. I should never have lied to you. I'm hopeless.'

'*I can't cope. I just can't cope,*' Batty agreed, bouncing up and down.

'You're not hopeless! You're the best, kindest, loveliest aunt in the whole world. And I've missed you.'

Stella ran to her and gave her a big hug.

'Oh Stella, I've missed you too, more than I can say.'

'Aren't you lonely in this lighthouse?'

'It's what I deserve.' Her aunt smiled bravely.

'Do you mean you like it here?'

'It's what I deserve,' she repeated, holding her tight.

Stella was puzzled by her reply, but something else puzzled her even more.

She released herself from her aunt's embrace, and stood back.

'You've changed, Aunt Zany. You look completely different.'

'Do I?'

'Yes. You look nice. I mean, you don't look so ill. But there's something else. Something... Yes! I know what it is! You didn't *rattle* when you stood up just now!'

Her aunt had, indeed, stopped making peculiar noises. Nor was she clinging onto pieces of furniture to remain upright. She was standing unaided, as straight and as poised as a pencil balanced on its end – with no visible means of support!

'My rattling days are over,' she boasted modestly. 'I thought I would die without my pills, but a curious thing happened. I felt better!'

'I want us to be friends again. Can we? Please.'

'I'd love to, my darling, but – ' She turned away from Stella. 'I'm afraid it's better that we don't see each other any more.'

'Why?' Stella asked, pouting.

'I'll explain one day, when you're older.'

Another voice made them jump.

'I know why.'

It was Mr Beeswax.

He was listening in the shadows of the open doorway. Just then, bright flashes of lightning caught his mild features, lending his face an unusually sinister look – the look of a man with a strange and terrible secret to reveal.

'I have a strange and terrible secret to reveal,' he said. 'The time has come for the truth.'

He closed the door quietly behind him.

'On the other hand, if I am wrong, my sincere apologies. Forthwith.'

Thunder crashed and banged as Aunt Zany paced up and down, wringing her hands.

'You promised to leave me alone, Mr Beeswax. I insist you go at once and take Stella with you. This is not the moment for strange and terrible secrets.'

'It is!' Stella insisted. 'A thunderstorm is the perfect time. I *love* strange and terrible secrets almost more than anything!' she declared, not entirely accurately.

'I will respect your wishes and leave as soon as one very important question is cleared up. Stella, you've noticed how much healthier your aunt looks?'

'Yes, like a completely different person.'

'There's nothing odd about that,' Aunt Zany protested. 'People recover. I stopped taking the pills.'

'Isn't there something else different, Stella? Look carefully.'

Aunt Zany presented the very picture of remorse, standing with her head slightly bowed and her hands clasped, as if about to say a prayer.

Stella tried to figure out what it was about Aunt Zany's appearance that had changed. A significant detail.

Her aunt hastily hid her hands behind her back.

Her hands...

'Yes! I know what it is! You're not wearing your brown mittens! They used to cover your painfully swollen knuckles. Let me see your hands, Aunt Zany.'

'No. Please.'

Mr Beeswax smiled sympathetically. 'It's for the best.'

Aunt Zany knew in her heart that Mr Beeswax's words were wise.

'Very well.'

Reluctantly, she showed Stella her hands.

'Your arthritis has gone. You told me it would *never* go. You said it's impossible to get rid of.'

There was a pause.

'Shall I tell her, or will you?' Mr Beeswax asked.

Aunt Zany opened her mouth, but nothing came out.

'Very well. I shall do it.'

More dazzling flashes of lightning danced about the room. This time, it was Aunt Zany's face that suddenly looked sinister.

'Stella, this lady – ' Mr Beeswax began.

'No,' Aunt Zany quietly interrupted him. 'Thank you, Mr Beeswax, but I think I should tell her.'

'By all means.'

'Tell me what?'

'Stella, I have a dreadful confession to make.'

'What is it?'

Outside, the wind screamed and wailed, like a horrible warning.

'Stella – I am not the person you think I am.'

'Of course you are. You're my Aunt Zany. You haven't changed that much.'

'No. I am not.'

'Well then – who are you?'

Thunder shook the whole lighthouse as if it were about to topple over and collapse into the waves.

'I am your mother.'

CHAPTER TWENTY-THREE

It Was Like This...

Ten minutes later, Stella and Mr Beeswax were sitting comfortably in front of the warm fire, sipping cocoa and munching oatmeal biscuits, their wet coats hung up and dripping onto old newspapers.

'Yes, it's true, Stella. I am your mother,' her ex-aunt continued, leaning guiltily against the mantelpiece.

'But before I explain, tell me, Mr Beeswax – when did you guess?'

'My suspicions were raised,' he began, 'on Wednesday the fifteenth of November last, at eleven twenty-two am precisely.'

He removed his glasses thoughtfully and wiped them on a clean handkerchief.

'As I approached your house, I was roused from my day-dreams by music of such unearthly loveliness, I dropped my briefcase.'

Stella cleverly turned her amused chuckle into a chesty cough.

'Someone was playing the cello. Could it be Stella? Surely a more mature musician. Maybe her teacher? Unable to stem my overwhelming curiosity, I peeped through the library window and I beheld a sight I shall never forget.'

He faced Stella's mother, his cheeks slightly pink with excitement.

'You were playing the yellow cello like an angel. In that moment, I fell permanently in love with you for the rest of my life. And you weren't wearing any mittens!'

He pulled himself together.

'Later, when the maid showed me into the drawing room, I complimented you on your performance. You became most agitated.

' '*What you heard, Mr Beeswax, was not music,*' you claimed, rather curiously, '*I was merely polishing the cello, not playing it.*' I was baffled. Polishing doesn't produce such beautiful sounds. If anything, perhaps an occasional squeak.

'But you insisted. '*How could I play any instrument with my painful arthritis?*' you demanded.

'And there, indeed, were your hands covered by your brown mittens once more. I was totally mystified.'

Stella's mother was looking very shamefaced for telling such porky-pies.

'Just then,' Mr Beeswax continued, 'Stella returned home from an important board meeting. As she entered the room, you hissed, '*Don't mention a word of this to Stella.*'

'Of course, I agreed, but I wondered what this could possibly mean.'

He gazed into the far distance, strangely moved.

'The next day, I foolishly asked you to marry me.'

'You did.'

'And you refused. You said that our paths must never cross again! '*Never!*' you cried. '*Never, never, never!*''

'I'll explain why in a moment. Go on.'

'Time passed. I was very unhappy. And very perplexed. Somehow, the mystery of it all seemed bound up in that yellow cello. I needed to find the answer.'

He paused, struggling to compose his features.

'All I knew for certain was that the cello had been left to Stella, several months earlier, in the will of a deceased lady called Olive Underfelt. The executor of the will had sent the cello to me. And so, according to his instructions, I delivered it to Stella.'

'That's how this whole story began,' Stella reflected aloud, blowing on her cocoa to cool it.

'Exactly! Remembering this, I decide to pay the executor a visit. He turned out to be a pleasant Swedish gentleman by the name of Hans Upp, a retired army general.

'"*Yes,*' he informed me, '*Olive Underfelt used to be my nearest neighbour. In those days I was living in Cornwall,*' he said. '*On a small island.*'"

'Called Small Island?' Stella asked shrewdly.

Mr Beeswax nodded.

'Correct. So I said to Mr Upp, '*Could you kindly give me her address?*' '*Of course,*' he replied, with a Swedish lilt. '*Blinking Rock Lighthouse, Cornwall.*'

'But when I consulted the Directory of British Lighthouses, it was listed under the name of Madagascar Wishbone – Stella's dead mother! And a gifted cellist!'

'Yes, that is my true name,' she admitted. 'I'm really Mad.'

'The moment I began to climb those stairs,' Mr Beeswax said, reliving every harrowing second, 'with the storm raging and the cello playing, it all suddenly came to me. Stella's mother and her aunt might somehow be one and the same person! It was impossible and yet true!

'The thought took my breath away! I was stunned! I stood absolutely still, rooted to the spot, unable to move or speak! On step forty-nine.'

'I thought he'd disappeared into thin air,' Stella muttered to her mother.

'Your aunt had given me a stern warning that we must never meet again. '*Never, never, never!*' But why? What was she hiding? The answer was waiting seventy-three more steps above... '

Mr Beeswax thoughtfully dunked his oatmeal biscuit into his cocoa.

'My torment seemed to last for an eternity. Then I heard Stella call out my name. Should I reply? No, I couldn't. Those warning words were ringing inside my head. '*Never, never, never!*' And yet I had to know. So I resumed climbing.'

Just as Mr Beeswax was about to eat his biscuit, the soaked bit fell back into his cocoa. Plop!

Stella's mother handed Mr Beeswax a teaspoon. He accepted with a grateful smile, then discreetly scooped the biscuit out of his cocoa and ate it. He gazed at her adoringly.

'And a few moments ago, as I was standing outside that door in the dark, I heard Stella ask if you were lonely living here. And you said something odd – 'It's what I *deserve.*'

'In a fraction of a second, I put two and two together, and the whole jigsaw puzzle fell into place! It wasn't Stella's aunt at all but her *mother* who had returned to this lighthouse – to punish herself for what she had done!'

'Yes, it *is* what I deserve. You guessed right.'

She touched Mr Beeswax on the arm, affectionately.

'Thank you, Basil, for that beautifully clear account. I'm very impressed.'

Mr Beeswax nearly fainted with pleasure and could only reply with what sounded like a muffled sneeze.

'You see, I did one bad thing and I've been paying for it ever since. And now,' she said, 'at long last, I can get it off my chest!'

She sat down in a chair facing Stella.

'Everything I told you was true – about growing up with my sister, Zany, in Africa and our coming to England. All true, except for one thing.

'Yes, we had very different characters. I was musical and witty, whereas Zany was clumsy and tone deaf. However, we looked and sounded exactly alike, because we were twin sisters. People were often unable to tell us apart.'

'What was the bad thing you did?' Stella asked solemnly.

'It was like this. Two years after you were born, I became fascinated by a plumber from Slough, called Rocky Bottom. I thought he liked me too, so I ran away with him, leaving you with your father. And I regretted it immediately.'

'*Silly idiot!*' exclaimed Batty.

'I *begged* your father to forgive me and let me come home, but he wouldn't. He said it was beyond a joke! He paid lawyers huge sums of money to make it illegal for me to contact you ever again! Otherwise I would go to jail. He even changed his will. It said:

> '*I leave all my money to my daughter, Stella, on one condition. Stella must never meet or speak to her mother again. Even if she bumps into her in the street by accident and she says 'Hallo, Mum!' all of Stella's money will be placed in a big pile on the back lawn and burnt to ashes.*'

She sighed sadly. 'He was very serious about it.'

'We call it the Bonfire Clause in the trade,' Mr Beeswax observed knowledgeably. 'A lot of rich people put it in their wills.'

'He told the servants that I had died changing a light bulb. They were strictly forbidden to mention my name thereafter, not because he mourned for me, but because he hated me. I felt so ashamed and miserable.

'Thank goodness your dear Aunt Zany kindly agreed to give up her job and take care of you. She'd had quite enough of bus conducting. I was deeply grateful to her. But oh – I missed you dreadfully!'

'So what did you do?'

'An unusual advert in the paper caught my eye: –

LIGHTHOUSE FOR SALE

The Perfect Place To Get Away From It All

(moderate lantern skills required)

'I instantly bought it under the name of Olive Underfelt, to escape from my wicked past. And because that's all there was on the floor. And here I sat in this room, month after month, sobbing and playing the cello to ease my sadness, with Batty flying round my head, repeating my cries of woe.'

'*Things couldn't possibly get worse,*' muttered Batty, sounding exactly like Stella.

'I became convinced that my heart would break. But if I should die of sorrow, I thought, what would happen to my beloved cello? And to Batty? So I wrote a will and left my dear parrot to Sandy Bottom and the yellow cello to you.

'A nice local gentleman agreed to be my executor – a retired Swedish army captain called Hans Upp. He was my closest neighbour but we were only on waving terms.'

'What happened then?' Stella urged her on, enjoying her mother's agonised confession.

'Well, four years passed, and then one day, out of the blue, I received a letter from your Aunt Zany.

'She said, '*You've got to come back. They are both driving me up the pole! I've had a marvellous idea. Why don't we change places? No one will guess!*'

'At first, I wasn't at all keen, but Zany insisted.

'She said, *'Look, you can't sit around playing that cello day after day. It's unhealthy. And you keep letting the lantern go out. All the boats are crashing into the rocks. It won't do. Your lighthouse sounds the ideal place for me. A bit of peace and quiet for a change!'*

'So I agreed to swap places with her. We worked out an ingenious but simple plan...

'One afternoon, Aunt Zany casually said to your father, *'I'm just popping round the corner to buy a jar of pickled onions.'* Half an hour later, Aunt Zany came back with the pickled onions. Except that it wasn't her, it was me! I had exchanged clothes with her inside the ladies' loo in Regent's Park. I even put on her pathetic brown mittens. And she was right – no one guessed.'

'I remember that day!' Stella exclaimed. 'All of a sudden you didn't know how to turn on the TV or where the soup spoons were kept or what my pet scorpion ate for supper.'

'Yes, I was completely flummoxed. So I pretended poor Aunt Zany was growing even more absent-minded than usual. You fell for it, thank goodness. But it only made you more bad-tempered than ever!'

'I suspected something was odd,' Stella recalled. 'You were very graceful all of a sudden, not tripping over carpets and bashing into doors. And every time I said, *'I need to go to the toilet,'* you burst into tears and hugged me.'

'I did. I couldn't bear to let you out of my sight for a single second. The whole experience was such agony, I got into the habit of swallowing pills to calm my nerves.'

'And you weren't half as strict with me as my real Aunt Zany.'

'It's true. Your appalling fits of rage overwhelmed me. I was completely unprepared. So I took even more pills. That's when I started rattling everywhere. But it was worth it, just to be close to you, as you screamed at the window cleaner and threw your socks at the maid.'

Stella bit her lip. 'I'm sorry I was so naughty.'

'Pretending I didn't know how to play my beloved cello was the hardest thing of all. I could hardly keep my hands off it. Mr Beeswax caught me playing one morning when you were out, as you've just heard. That nearly gave the game away! During the day was no good, I realised. So at midnight, when you were fast asleep, I used to take it into my bedroom and run through a few pieces, just to keep in practice.'

'I heard the music in my sleep. I thought I was dreaming!'

'And when you were determined to sell your cello, I did all I could to encourage you to keep it and to take lessons. The thought of it being smashed to bits at a rock concert horrified me!'

'So *you're* the one who broke into Paul Quickly's van and brought the cello back.'

Her mother shook her head, smiling mischievously.

'I didn't need to. When I explained the situation to Mr Quickly, he said, '*No prob, Miss 'Andlebar. Lets 'ave a bit a fun with young Stella.*' He made up that silly story about your cello vanishing from his van. In fact, it never even left the house!'

She had to laugh.

'He is such a good sport!'

Stella was so shocked, her mouth fell wide open.

'Grown-ups always say it's wrong to tell a lie.'

'Of course it is!' her mother hastily agreed. 'You should never tell a lie.'

She gave Mr Beeswax a quick glance. He looked up at the ceiling as if his mind was elsewhere.

'Unless,' she whispered, leaning furtively towards Stella, 'you do it for a very good reason and no one gets hurt. Then it's all right.'

Stella was not at all convinced by her mother's free and easy way with truth-telling. She frowned her disapproval.

However, her mother cleared her throat and resumed recounting her sensational story.

'Where was I? Oh yes. And so, just to be near you and love you, I carried on being your Aunt Zany. But the strain – oh the strain!' She shook her head.

'And your poor Aunt Zany wasn't at all happy in the lighthouse. Her last letter to me was so pathetic.

"*These stairs are too much for me,*' she wrote, '*even worse than on the buses! I can't cope! I just can't cope!*'

'When dear Zany died, I was sorely tempted to tell you the truth. But if I'd dared to admit that I was in fact your mother, all your money would've gone up in smoke. And I knew how much it meant to you.

'And when Mr Beeswax asked me to marry him, I wanted to so much but I couldn't.'

'Why?'

'Because I was a complete fake! Impersonating my own dead sister! It would have been very unfair on him. Not to mention illegal. When you sent me away, I decided it was for the best.'

'You said you were going to Africa.'

'That was my original plan, but I soon discovered I couldn't afford the ticket for such a long journey. So I came back here and lived alone, as before. And Batty flew back too! Suddenly one morning, there he was, flapping and squawking outside the window. He's been lovely company for me.'

'Why is there a for sale sign outside?'

'Since your Aunt Zany died, I've been trying to sell this lighthouse but no one wants to buy it because it costs a fortune to redecorate.'

'So it was my *real* Aunt Zany who died here?'

'Yes. Poor Zany. She had hated working as a bus conductor, stumbling up and down those stairs all day with a parrot on her shoulder, collecting fares. Stairs and fares! Perhaps a lighthouse with a hundred and twenty-two steps wasn't the ideal place for her to retire.'

Stella considered the whole story for a moment.

'Why did you run away with that plumber from Slough?'

'Because I fell in love with him.'

'Why?'

Her mother sighed and shrugged her shoulders.

'Ask the storm outside why it suddenly blows up. I simply found him very nice to be with.'

'Why?'

'Because he was kind to me and I was unhappy.'

'Why?'

'Because I didn't love your father.'

'Why?'

'Because he wouldn't speak to me.'

'Why?'

'Because we weren't suited to each other.'

'Why?'

'Oh Stella, when you're older you'll understand there isn't always a good reason for what we do or feel and, consequently, we make mistakes.'

'But I *do* understand,' Stella nodded wisely. 'I thought Mr Steele was my best friend. And I was wrong.'

'Oh dear, I'm extremely sorry to hear that. But not altogether surprised.'

'One more question. Is everyone in our family completely barmy?'

'We are odd, it has to be admitted.'

Stella put down her cup of cocoa, got up from her chair and sat on her mother's lap. She gazed closely into her eyes.

'I'm glad you're my real mother.'

'So am I. Can you forgive me, Stella?'

'Yes. On one condition. Do you promise never to go away again?'

'Oh yes, my darling, *of course* I do! I promise!'

'Even if Mr Beeswax asks you to marry him again, and you change your mind this time and say yes?'

'Oh I *do* promise, *especially* if Mr Beeswax asks me to marry him again and this time I say yes.'

She smiled at Mr Beeswax, who dropped his plate of biscuits on the floor.

'I think it's a very sensible idea,' Stella advised, like a no-nonsense bank manager. 'Because then we could all live together. And I can still learn the cello and go to PING.'

She put her arms around her mother's neck, hugged her tightly and yawned.

'I think it's a very sensible idea too, my darling,' her mother said, giving Stella a kiss on her cheek, 'but it's impossible.'

'Why?' Stella demanded, unable to stop her eyelids drooping. She was feeling weary and a bit grumpy by now.

'Because, my darling, when you marry someone, you have to give your real name. And if I did that, everyone would know who I was. And then you would lose all your money on the spot! Every single penny! You wouldn't be too happy about that.'

'All my money... ' Stella repeated, with a sleepy smile.

'Yes, it would be piled up on the lawn and burnt, according to the Bonfire Clause in your father's will.'

She hugged her daughter protectively and kissed her cheek.

'But never mind, my love; we'll sort something out. Tell me, what happened when you flew to Vienna to buy that big diamond? I imagine you're richer than ever now.'

Mr Beeswax cleared his throat in a helpful manner.

'Stella,' he said quietly, 'shall I explain your present situation to your mother, forthwith? Or will you?'

No answer.

Stella had fallen asleep and was having another extraordinary dream about her yellow cello.

And that is the end of the story.

Or is it?

CHAPTER TWENTY-FOUR

A Curse and a Coincidence

Not quite. When Stirling Steele disappeared at the airport, a man with orange hair and a black moustache called Al Beano emerged from the gents' and boarded a plane for France.

Guess who.

In Paris, he booked into a cheap hotel under the name of Herbie Vorr. Interpol then chased Mr Steele (yes, you guessed right) all over Europe, until he began to run out of disguises and fake passports.

These bore names such as:

    Cash de Spencer,
    Lance Boyles,
    Stan de Teeze,
    Clement Morning,
    Mayor Culper,
    Kurt Snubb,
    Peter Owt,
    Ewan Ooze-Armi,
    Perry Winkle,
    Benny Fitz,
    Hugh Mungus, and
    Frank X Change.

He even had passports in which he claimed to be:

    Polly Ester,
    Mo Mentum,
    Anne Droyd,
    Isla Doggs,
    Annette Proffit,
    Lynn C Doyle,

Faye Tallity,
Ella Fantyne, and
Victoria Spunge.

Finally, dodging the police by the skin of his teeth, he managed to reach Switzerland. There, wearing dark-skinned makeup, he stayed at a youth hostel calling himself Philip Eannoh.

Later that night, he stole a hot-air balloon in which he aimed to sail over the Alps to his freedom. Or so he thought.

Carrying the Cripes Diamond in a rucksack on his back, he climbed into the balloon's gondola and hastily removed his disguise with face-cream. He then untied the mooring rope, enjoying a self-satisfied laugh at the ingenuity of his plan.

'Ha ha ha!'

The airship rose up and up into a sky festooned with millions of the biggest and most dazzling diamonds in all creation. Stirling Steele's teeth and eyes sparkled almost as brightly.

'Ha ha ha!'

His plan was working perfectly. However, there is a very wise old proverb that says: '*Pride goes before a fall.*'

Mr Steele had made one serious mistake. He had failed to realise that the Cripes Diamond was rather like him. A fraud.

It was *not* absolutely pure, as experts had claimed. The reason for the vivid colours that flashed from its centre was – an internal flaw. Yes, some stunningly beautiful diamonds contain a very small, weak point. This indicates a severe strain within the structure which can, under certain circumstances, even cause the diamond to explode.

This can be triggered when, for example, the stone is warmed inside the pocket of a would-be thief. Or when there is a change in atmospheric pressure...

As the balloon rose higher and higher above the snowy Alps, Stirling Steele leaned out over the edge of the gondola to observe the faint lights of a village glimmering way below.

A breeze ruffled his blond hair as if to say, 'You clever rascal. You have a charmed life.'

Stirling Steele was so pleased with himself, he puffed out his manly chest.

'Yes, I *am* clever and I *do* have a charmed life! Ha ha ha!'

His ribcage had swelled by several inches. However, unknown to him, the air pressure inside the diamond had also increased...

As the flattering breeze wafted him past the spectacular peak of the Eiger Mountain, he opened the top of his rucksack to get a sandwich.

The precious gem sparkled in the brilliant starlight.

Mr Steele could not resist its fascination. Taking the diamond out of the bag, he held it up before his eyes like a fabulous trophy. At that very moment, the diamond exploded with astonishing violence, shattering into a million tiny, worthless fragments.

A cloud of glittering diamond dust momentarily blinded Stirling Steele. He lost his balance and toppled over the edge of the gondola.

Desperate to save himself from falling, his arms flailed wildly about. He just managed to grab hold of a guide-rope with one hand and he clung on to it as tightly as possible.

And there he dangled in the midnight starry blackness, the same flattering breeze swinging him to and fro.

He might still have been safe, but in his haste he had failed to wipe all the greasy makeup remover from his fingers. He suddenly realised that the only thing keeping him airborne – one thin piece of rope – was beginning to slip very slowly through his grasp.

He looked up and watched in horror as his hand began to slide down the rope, inch by inch. He tried with all his strength to tighten his grip. But in vain.

In a few agonising seconds, he reached the end of his rope.

And true to the stone's terrible curse, Mr Steele fell to a tumbling, screaming death hundreds of feet below in a goat pasture.

The Cripes Diamond had claimed its final agonised victim.

No goats were hurt in the telling of this story.

And in case you were wondering, Robin Banks did *not* receive a knighthood. For this reason:

After his lively conversation with Stella, he stomped home in a bad temper, and made unnecessarily rude remarks about his wife's face. She heard every single word because he was shouting at her across the dinner table.

He had chosen the wrong moment. His wife, Paris Banks, happened to be feeling out of sorts that evening.

'That's it,' she decided. 'Enough is enough.'

A few minutes later, the police received an anonymous tip-off from a woman about a crooked property deal Mr Banks had masterminded. She also gave the precise whereabouts of two of his business rivals.

When the bodies were dug up, a jury at the Old Bailey agreed that Mr Banks should enjoy a more restrained lifestyle for the next thirty years. Minimum.

To end, I feel I ought to show you this letter which I received yesterday. It might clear up one or two points.

Dear Mr Gale,

My name is Stella Wishbone and I have just read your story about me, which you wrote without my permission. I don't think I was that naughty, but when I asked my mother if I was she said no comment.

How did you know so much about me? Were you one of my servants? Anyway, I just wanted to say something. Your story contains a few mistakes.

First of all, there is no such thing as a Bonfire Clause. I looked it up. Maybe there should be.

Also, a commander in the Royal Navy cannot use his ship as if it were a minicab. Giving people lifts to lighthouses would never be allowed. His vessel is supposed to operate exclusively on official navy business. (I hope you don't get Commander Ableforce into trouble with his superiors.)

What's more, he told me that only officers are piped aboard ship, otherwise it could go on all day and people would get completely fed up with it.

Oh, and by the way, I know for a fact that children are not permitted to make bids at public auctions, mainly because we tend to fidget with our hands and auctioneers could become horribly confused.

You were right about King Henry VIII, though. It sounds unlikely, but he *really did* own an African Grey Parrot. Thank goodness it never said '*Silly idiot*' to Henry, otherwise its little head might well have been chopped off.

As for Batty's name – yes, the Swahili word for lucky is *bahati*. And the Limba Claire Tree really does grow in Africa, just as you described, and its wood is a lovely gold colour. I am looking at my yellow cello now as I write this.

My mother and Mr Beeswax were married recently so technically I'm not an excitable waif any more, but I am still allowed to go to PING.

Someone told me that PING bears a striking resemblance to another London orphanage also founded by a sea captain, but his name was Thomas Coram. He was a very kind-hearted gentleman and his home for abandoned children was called The Foundling Hospital. It closed ages ago but my mother took me to see pictures of it at the Foundling Museum in Brunswick Square. Well worth a visit. Nearest tube Russell Square.

As for that Cripes Diamond!

I did a bit of research on the subject. All the scientific facts about diamonds listed in that magazine article are *completely true*. But I still think those stories about the Cripes Diamond being cursed were made up by someone. And here is why.

Have you heard of the Hope Diamond? It's very famous for being cursed. Terrible things are supposed to happen to anyone who owns it or even touches it!

The story goes that there was once an old statue of an Indian goddess called Sita, and she wore a beautiful big blue diamond in her crown. She was very powerful because her husband was the chief Hindu god, Rama.

A stupid merchant decided to steal the diamond and Sita was not well pleased. The man ran off with it to Russia, thinking he had escaped unpunished, but one night he got lost in a forest and was torn to pieces by wild dogs.

Years after, it belonged to King Louis XVI of France and his wife Queen Marie Antoinette, and they were both guillotined in the French Revolution in 1793.

In 1839 it was named after Mr Henry Hope whose whole family went completely bankrupt. Then in 1911, a lady called Mrs Evalyn McLean bought it. Her little boy died in a car accident;

her daughter killed herself and her husband was declared insane. Talk about one thing after another.

There's only one problem with this scary legend. None of it is true. The whole curse idea was cooked up, possibly by a jeweller called Pierre Cartier. A clever sales pitch. And it worked!

That's why I definitely do NOT believe in the Curse of the Cripes Diamond. Except, maybe, for one strange coincidence.

It might interest you to know that when the Cripes Diamond exploded and Mr Steele fell out of the balloon, that was the exact same moment that I fell asleep on my mother's lap in the lighthouse. And I have a theory that the Cripes Diamond's famous curse evaporated then too, because nothing awful has happened to me since. Touch wood!

And just so you know, I said I would create a wildlife reserve for my friend Sandy and I *did*. This is how:

A newspaper editor wrote to me saying, 'Would you give our readers a heartbreakingly frank account of your riches to rags ordeal?' He offered to pay me quite a tidy sum!

I asked my mum if this would be all right. At first, she was concerned that my greedy old ways had popped up again, but the money wasn't for me.

Half of it I gave to my mum and stepdad to re-decorate the lighthouse.

The other half went on making Sandy's dream come true. The Sandy Bottom Wildlife Centre near Warblerswick provides eighty acres of protected woodland for birds to live and breed in safety.

There was an official opening in the local village hall with conjuring tricks and ice cream. Mrs Bottom was the guest of honour, and gave a speech about how Sandy would have been a wonderful ornithologist, and then Annie Clipps and I played a duet specially composed by Annie, called The Woodpecker Waltz. I think it's fantastic.

Wanda Backenforth sat in the very front row wearing a huge green and orange hat. Half way through, I peeked at her and she gave me a thumbs up.

When it ended, everyone clapped and said, 'What a nice tune. I'll be humming that all day now.' But I noticed that my mum's cheeks were wet with tears.

'Did I play wrong notes?' I asked.

'Far from it,' she replied. 'People don't always cry because they're unhappy.'

Grown-ups are so peculiar.

When we got home, I said, 'Isn't it funny? I thought that losing all my money would be a disaster. But things have turned out really well.'

My mum agreed. 'It was a blessing in disguise,' she said, 'and a surprisingly jolly one.' And then she added, 'All things considered.'

I knew she was thinking about Sandy. So was I.

My stepdad nodded and said, 'It's true. Things sometimes turn out better in ways we can't even begin to imagine.'

And then my mother smiled at him and he dropped his toasted muffin.

Yours sincerely,
Stella Wishbone

THE END